My Clingy Girlfriend

My Clingy Girlfriend

MADHURI BANERJEE

𝓌

westland ltd

61, II Floor, Silverline Building, Alapakkam Main Road, Maduravoyal, Chennai 600095

93, I Floor, Sham Lal Road, Daryaganj, New Delhi 110002

First published by westland ltd 2015

10 9 8 7 6 5 4 3 2

ISBN: 978-93-84030-89-6

Typeset in Californian FB by SÜRYA, New Delhi
Printed at Thomson Press (India) Ltd.

For Bala: Thank you for encouraging me to go beyond my comfort zone. Without your love, support and inputs, this book would not have been possible.

For my brothers: Ani, Taju Dada, Bujum Dada, Bubam, Babush, Chotu, Jadu. And my dad – Dhrubo, who is my hero. And to Gopal Uncle who always keeps me in splits.

Cheers to the Bengali roots!

For Ariaana – My sweetest treasure. My proudest accomplishment. I wish the best for you always and pray you will become a wonderful lady.

1

I can honestly say that I, Obrokranti Banerjee, know jack shit about love. Nothing. Nada. Zip. Yet I am in a relationship. It is actually the most intense relationship I have ever been in after my mother who finally let me go out into the world alone at the age of twenty-five. But then you can't blame my mother. All Bengali moms think their sons are Jesus Christ and they themselves are the Virgin Mary.

The thing is that most Bengali men don't know a thing about women. I am no different. When I finally started working in Mumbai and met this beautiful woman, I immediately proposed using the only pick-up line I knew: 'Is there an airport nearby, or is that just my heart taking off?' She laughed so much that we became friends in an instant. When I proposed a few hours later, asking if she wanted to be my girlfriend, she immediately said yes. I should have known something was fishy right then. We were both four drinks down at a kid's birthday party and neither of us knew what we were getting into.

But here I am two years later with the same girl and things are great. Just great. Yup. Great.

Who am I kidding? They're not great. My girlfriend is a

psycho. She is the clingiest girlfriend in the world. Space and time as a concept do not exist for her. She wants to be with me all the time. She stalks me. She hounds me. She wants my world to revolve around her. She's utterly and completely mad. Yet I cannot let go of her. Why? Because I'm bloody scared.

Two reasons. One I might never have a girlfriend again, and a robust, young Bengali man like me needs to show off to his peers that he can have any woman he wants. Even though, deep down, I know it was a fluke. Second, because I need to beat that idiot cousin of mine Shubir, who has so many women flocking to him all because he looks like a *bhadrolok* at the *pujo pandals* every October. I mean, I did try, but somehow my dhoti kept flying up, making a caricature out of me. So I decided to stick to wearing jeans and a kurta at the *pandals*, and the Bengali women have never looked at me after that. I mean no self-respecting Bengali wears jeans. At pujo.

Therefore, I am stuck with one woman as compared to Shubir who has a harem of them.

My clingy girlfriend does love me though. She cooks for me. She cares for me. She asks me where I am and what I do on a regular basis. Almost fifty to sixty times a day. And she always accompanies me to all events – official, personal, even boys' night out. A boys' night out should mean a man can get away from his female partner to go out drinking with his guy friends. But she insists on coming along, saying she hasn't met them for a long time either. Ideally, the two should never mix. Keep the woman in your life separate from your male friends. There's a disaster waiting to happen right there.

Recently my friends have been too busy to have a boys'

night. I've called them a couple of times, and could hear some loud rock music and laughter in the background when one of them said they were working. I wonder if they were lying?

I have thought about leaving my girlfriend. But then I might never have sex again. I mean with a real girl. There are only so many Sunny Leone videos I can download. My hard drive is on the verge of collapsing. And she really is good in bed. My girlfriend I mean, not Sunny. Sunny, I know I will have one day, as soon as I have the courage to use my pick-up lines on her. But sometimes I have to stop myself from screaming out Sunny's name in bed and quickly use my super-brain to change it to my girlfriend's, Radha, and it comes out as a hiss like Sss – radha and she always gets mad if I'm thinking of someone else. This is when I say, 'No baby, I was moaning in pleasure and then said your name.' Hehe. She buys it.

Some things my super-brain can't quite figure out though. Every time I get back from the bathroom, I see my phone's display glowing. Sometimes, I could have sworn I had certain messages from my female colleagues in my inbox, but they're gone when I check later. Sometimes my mother says she called but I didn't pick up. And it's not even in my missed call list. Ma thinks I'm making excuses, but honestly, I would never ignore my mother. I worship her. She's always been the first woman in my life and will remain so. I think Radha is a little jealous of that fact. She wants to be the first, second and last woman ever for me. God, how I feel caged!

I make sure I never miss a call from Radha, though. Because if I do, she'll land up in my office. 'Baby, I thought you'd died. I was so concerned,' she said one day when I was in a meeting. My colleagues didn't let me live it down for the entire week.

So I always pick up Radha's call. No matter what I'm doing. I still have the liberty to ignore my mother's. Sometimes.

I know Radha is possessive. But then who is not in this world? Every relationship is fucked up. Shubir, my cousin, who is also known as Lengtu, was in a relationship where his girlfriend almost forced him to get married. It was then that he came up with a brilliant plan. The *kundli*. Now, whenever he wants to break up with a girl, he tells her, 'Darling, I would happily spend the rest of my life with you, but my punditji says our *kundlis* don't match. And I can never go against our punditji. It's just bad karma for both of us.' Indian girls understand: nothing matches the power of a matched *kundli*. Even though half a dozen of them end up divorced later. But then, that's not the parents' problem. At least they matched the *kundli*. Goddamn Lengtu has fooled about twenty women like this. The rest were mutual separations. Even the girl couldn't stand his chauvinistic ways after a few days.

I once tried the *kundli* story with Radha. She said she would match it with her punditji and came back with the result that we were a faultless twenty on twenty. Perfect match. Why am I not surprised.

Don't get me wrong. I *am* somewhat happy to have Radha in my life. Although, sometimes I wish she were more independent. She is a housewife, you see. Even though we aren't married yet. She says she's preparing for the role. She sits in my house the whole day long and orders the maid around. And if the maid isn't cleaning properly, she calls me in office so I can also scream at her. This is also what she does with plumbers, carpenters, drivers, electricians, internet-walas, newspaper boys, the milkman, vegetable vendors, car cleaners, and the tailor. She will immediately call and say, 'Baby! The tailor is saying he can't deliver my blouse by tomorrow. Tell him to do it!' And then hand him the phone. And I will then lower my voice, since I am invariably in the middle of an office meeting, and speak to her tailor about a blouse that she needs for God knows what reason by tomorrow. But that's my job. To make her life easier. Otherwise she'll make my life hell.

I know my colleagues think that our relationship is strange, but really, it's fine. After all, I am the master of the house. And she waits for me to come home before she goes out anywhere. Which I think is very dutiful of her. Though this means that, most of the time, I have to rush back so that we can go out for groceries, or for dinner or to meet people or to shop for her. By people, I mean her friends and family. I have not met my mother now for a year. She doesn't let me go to Kolkata to meet her. She starts crying whenever I start making a plan. Then I have to make some excuse to my mother. My mother has threatened to visit anytime now. Haha. Then we shall see the fireworks. And I will leave both of them to sort it out for themselves and go out for my much-needed boys' night out.

Radha reads a lot. She reads books the entire day. She says she doesn't remember after a while what she has read, because she reads so much. However, whenever I want something my way, she quotes a line from some classic that makes me relent. One day I asked her which classic she was quoting from, and she said, 'Oh you know, Dickens.' And since I've read Dickens, I thought I could try and remember which character and we could play a guessing game. So I asked, 'Which novel?' And she just glared at me and said, 'All of them!'

I try not to piss her off too much. She is a beautiful creature. With long brown hair that reaches her waist and sparkling brown eyes, she is the epitome of Ma Durga. She just wants to banish all that is bad in my life. That's why I have tried to give up cigarettes. I smoke only in office and before I get home. On weekends, I go for a long walk and smoke. Later I pop a whole box of mints and pray hard that she doesn't catch me.

The smoking is a result of being in a very high-pressure job. Marketing for a flop channel is tough. We started off being a page 3 'lifestyle' channel, and right now we just have music and one reality show that's trying to run on shock value. There are dozens of 'programming' people who try to think of new ways to ruin the channel, and there's us in the marketing department, who shoot down their ideas.

The channel doesn't allow me to flourish to my true potential. Either it is a money problem or it's a poorly-made program problem. It's impossible to function creatively and use all my talent when I have such restraints. I am surrounded by nincompoops. The programming head comes up with weird show ideas, and since he has the CEO by his balls, he uses up the entire channel's money making stupid programs. For example, to add variety, they decided to do a show which had a man and a parrot answering questions on love from the audience. I mean that's utterly absurd. How does any man know anything about relationships? Stupid. And the parrot once said 'Fuck you', which we had to beep out. Seriously.

I can't take the pressure sometimes. The marketing head is in cohorts with the programming head and together they're conspiring to overthrow the CEO and take over the channel themselves. As advised by the parrot. No kidding. So anyone who opposes either of them gets the boot. And if we don't say anything, then the show flops and we're blamed for not marketing it properly. It's just too much. Once I came up with the idea that we should have a quiz show about our rich history with the super-brains of the country like Siddhartha Basu and Derek O'Brien. Have two people pitted against each other in every episode. Obviously, my idea was too intellectual for the idiots running this channel. 'We would need someone glamorous to host it then,' said the programming head. 'Someone intelligent too,' said the marketing head. 'Priyanka Chopra!' they yelled simultaneously. Then they said it would be too expensive to get her, and they dropped the idea. Idiots.

So, for now, I am going to just go along with whatever my bosses say. I'm turning twenty-eight next month. I hope things will change then. My family astrologer says a momentous change will occur in my life after I turn twenty-eight. My mother has been waiting for it eagerly. She even made me wear a pokhraj ring for success and a gomedh to control my *rahu*. I can feel it working every day. Success is around the corner. And sex too. But I'll get to that soon.

2

When I woke up this morning, Radha was already up and sitting in a corner with a cup of tea. She refused to talk to me. When I asked her what was wrong, she said, 'Nothing.' So I continued to read the paper and quickly finished my cereal. She refused to make me eggs and toast this morning, choosing instead to give me a dirty glare. I asked her again what was wrong and this time she said, 'You should know!' How would I know? I just woke up. And going by last night's hectic activity, I would have thought my stupendous stamina would have satisfied her for at least twenty-four hours.

I left for office rather quickly and didn't have time to check again. Many things were on my mind. Today the marketing and programming departments were headed to Resort hotel on Madh island for a conference. We were going to spend the night there, continue the meeting the next day and then all of us would depart in the evening. This is the so-called fun part of my job known as 'brain storming'. AKA 'mental masturbation'. I had mentioned this to Radha a few weeks ago and she had acted very strangely about it, begging me to come home since she couldn't sleep alone at night and was afraid of the dark. Now that's ridiculous. A grown woman who is afraid of the dark? It's like saying the royal Bengal tiger is afraid of the jungle.

While I was riding to Resort hotel, I could feel my phone vibrating furiously in my pocket. By the time I reached, I saw that Radha had sent me seventy-five messages explaining why she hadn't wanted to say anything in the morning. God, that woman can type a whole lot of shit. If you're going to say 'Nothing', then you should bloody well shut up after that. But she continued with how I was an insensitive knob who didn't care about how she felt and had gone off without even checking if she was okay. Um, hello! Didn't I say, 'I would have loved to have your eggs this morning,' before I left? That's supposed to mean I love you! Seriously, women are from another planet. We just put up with them for sex.

So, anyway, I called Radha to ask what had happened and she said, 'I had a dream about you with another woman and it freaked me out.'

Fact: most women at some point in their lives have had *a dream* about their man with another woman and then gotten angry about it. They will then be pissed off the entire day, and not speak to the man or will scream at him for a small little thing that they would generally ignore. Like, 'You've left your wet towel on the bed again? I cannot live with this shit anymore. I can't believe you're so insensitive to my feelings. You don't see me as a person at all. No wonder you're willing to cheat on me.'

And really, it won't even be about your towel. And the man will have no idea where that came from. Dreams, my friend. Beware of them.

Women are always insecure about their man going after another girl. And it's actually just that which drives us to the other woman. If a woman were confident of herself and trusted the man, she would know that he chose her because he thinks she's the one he wants to be with. Instead, she'll have dreams and become suspicious.

I assured Radha very quickly that it would never happen (in dreams and in real life as well) and I was devoted to her. But before I could hang up she started howling and I had to calm her down. Where are the bloody girl friends to look after your woman when you need them, I say? She is supposed to talk to her friends about this stuff. I took a deep breath and asked her, 'Why would I go with anyone else when I have the most beautiful creature with me?'

She said, 'In my dream, you wanted to sleep with someone thinner and had begun flirting with Kiran and then ended up in bed.' She continued to cry. Now excuse me for taking a moment to picture this myself, and get a hop. I haven't been with another woman for two years now, and this fantasy had never crossed my mind until she planted it! Though I wouldn't be surprised if Kiran had had that fantasy of me. I've seen her looking at me several times. I know my intellectual manliness is a big turn on for the ladies.

When I took a moment extra to respond, she became infuriated and said, 'This is not the answer I wanted! You are so out of tune with me.'

'Baby, chill now. We'll discuss it when I get back,' I said, while wondering why I was still standing outside Resort hotel with a bag at my feet instead of having checked in, and relaxing alone in a room with this vision of Kiran.

She continued to sob.

I pointed out one minor detail that she was forgetting: 'Radha, darling...this was a *dream. Your* dream. It wasn't real.'

Radha's voice took on a very high pitch. 'Dreams are a manifestation of some act that is carried out in daily life. I read it in a book.'

I immediately made a mental note to burn the book if I ever found it. I said, 'I promise to behave myself from now on.'

(Great insight – I always behave badly for four days every month. Every month. Period.)

'How?' Radha asked.

I sighed and said what every man says to keep the only woman who is willing to give him sex in his life happy, 'I will do whatever you want.'

I could hear a sigh at the other end, and then Radha said more cheerfully, 'Will you come home to me tonight then?'

Home? Why should I go home? This was a legitimate excuse for me to spend the night out drinking and singing with the boys. I hadn't practised my old Hindi songs for so long and I knew that after the conference we would all be down a few pegs and wouldn't mind each other's off-tune voices belting out Kishore Kumar numbers. I didn't want to go home. I had to think of a reasonable excuse quickly.

'Baby,' I said in my sweetest tone even though my masculine Bengaliness has given me a deep, resonating voice that makes the women go weak in the knees. 'It's mandatory for us to stay here. It's all for team bonding. The boss will not allow me to leave.' Radha insisted that she speak to the boss, but I said that since the conference had started, and I was already late by an hour because I was chatting with her, he would get even angrier. Radha made me promise that I would call her as soon as we had a tea break in another hour to discuss this. Since it was the only way she would hang up, I promised.

Needless to say, the first session of the conference didn't go too well for me. With visions of me making mad passionate love to Kiran and figuring out how to get out of going home for the night, I couldn't concentrate too much on what was being said. Raghav, the idiot marketing head, threw a chalk at me and asked me where my brain was. If I had told him, his brain would have reached there as well. Kiran is definitely hot and definitely thinner than Radha. Instead, I told Raghav I had an upset tummy and needed to be excused to use the toilet.

Crapping is the best excuse you can give another man. No woman gets this. If a man needs to crap, he is excused from anything. Only men understand *that pressure.* And you don't want to stink up a conference room with your day-old gas. You're always allowed to get up and leave to go shit even if you are meeting the prime minister who, I'm sure, goes several times of the day to get away from the people around him.

The loo is where a man can finally be alone. From girlfriends, bosses, work, life, and whatever is going on, to just be free with his shit. Literally. Those peaceful moments are few in a man's life, and God understands this. That's why he made men's metabolism better than women's. So we could spend more time in the bathroom, away from the opposite sex.

When I had cleared my system of all personal issues, I went back to the conference ready to dazzle them with my intelligence. The marketing and the programming head, Raghav and Ramesh, who I like to call the Tweedledee and Tweedledum of our organization, were going on about how we needed to change the vision of the company by modifying its brand offering. Like it can happen overnight! If Nike suddenly decides to not be a sports company but sell sanitary napkins, you think women will buy the product and with 'JUST DO IT' to boot? It's not so easy. What were these idiots talking about? This was a waste of time. I honestly felt that we should just call it quits and head straight to the bar to drink. After all, I had to head back for the night because my clingy girlfriend couldn't sleep alone in the dark.

The first session lasted a little longer than usual because everyone had made high-flying power point presentations (called decks) that lasted over the five-minute timeline given just to show what great dudes they were at it. They'd added videos and many semi-nude photos of Bollywood heroines that kept Tweedledee and Tweedledum on the slides even longer. So, the tea break came a whole two hours later instead of just one.

I quickly ran out to call Radha as she had given me forty-five missed calls by then. She answered after half a ring. 'I was going to call the police!'

'I'm so sorry, baby,' I said apologizing immediately so we wouldn't waste any time on why I was supposed to be sorry.

'WHO THE HELL WERE YOU SLEEPING WITH?' she screamed back at me.

I tried to explain to her that the session took longer than usual but she wouldn't listen. She asked again, who I was in bed with, and I was tempted to say Kiran but then stopped myself. My super-brain realized fast enough that it would lead to more trouble if I were sarcastic rather than continuously apologetic.

'Did you know I was feeling insecure?'

'Yes, baby.'

'Did you know I wanted to talk to you?

'Yes, baby.' Men need to sound like a broken record for women to forgive them. Any logic, arguments or questioning back could result in broken bones for the man.

'Did you know I needed reassurance?'

'Yes, baby.'

'Then why didn't you call when you said you would? Tell me the truth.'

I felt like I was on an interrogation stand, and honestly, I wanted to yell back Colonel Jessup's line from the film *A Few Good Men*. 'You can't handle the truth!' I wanted to say. 'You don't want the truth because deep down in places you don't talk about at parties, you want me on that wall, you need me on that wall.' Same tone. I thought I could pull it off. Radha would kill me if I made a joke now, though. Women want a man with a sense of humour, but refuse to see the funny side when they show it.

So instead, I desperately tried to comfort her using the same words I had so many times: 'Baby you know I love you. I'm so sorry. It will never happen again,' and added, 'I couldn't help it. Those nincompoops just kept going on and on about how the company needs to be something else.'

'So you couldn't message me? Your fingers were also paying attention to them?'

Now here's the thing. Most men's brains freeze up during an argument with the woman in their life. While a woman can and will lucidly rant about her feelings, the man will not be able to say a thing. And then when she screams at him to 'say something', all he can come up with are the things that he vaguely remembers from previous arguments.

I'm convinced studying for the tenth boards is a way to help men mug up standard sentences to say to women in adulthood. This rote system of education was invented just for brain-dead men. It saves us from saying anything foolish and managing to get some extra time until the grey cells kick in again.

The only way she would hang up was if I promised I would go back for the night after the conference. There went my drinking session. I hung up, and by this time, the second part of the session had almost started. I hadn't even had a chance to have tea and those lovely mini sandwiches and samosas that were served.

I was now ravenous. Bengalis should never be hungry. Never. They become like Bengal tigers hunting for prey. In human terms, they become angry, cranky, snappish, irritated, and more intolerable than they generally are. This goes for both men and women. A way to a Bengali's heart is to give him great food. Not a nutritious diet program. Bengalis have no custom where they need to fast. We do not believe in starving ourselves for the welfare of someone else. Teej, navratras, shravan – these are never celebrated by Bengalis. And even if they marry into a community that follows these festivals, they will find a way to sneak in some food during the day so they don't get a headache and die from starvation. The biggest Bengali celebration – Durga Puja (*pujos*) – is all about what *bhog* we're going to have and how many *mishtis* we've downed.

So when I went back into the conference room, I was pissed. My stomach was growling, and the fact that my evening plans were busted didn't help. I had nothing to lose when I started my presentation. I was ready to chew people alive!

3

My presentation was going to be different from the rest. I was told to explain with data why our television programs in the last quarter had failed. My PPT (AKA, the deck) had slides on each of the programs and research on why they hadn't taken off. I began with a powerful statement, 'Seven shows were launched in the last quarter. Out of them, five were flops!' I had meant to say 'didn't do well', but the hunger pangs were making my temper rise, and when my temper rises, I don't mince words.

'Let's start with the first one, the skimpily clad anchor talking about Bollywood classical songs. This has done so badly because it was scheduled at the same time as *Bigg Boss*, which has always had high ratings. Also, families are watching at this time, and they don't want to see old Bollywood songs. So no sponsor wants to come on board.' In a nutshell, I wanted to say, the jackass that came up with the concept probably borrowed an idea from a porn channel, and then decided to put it on prime time television. But I need my job so I managed to stop myself. I continued giving them facts and figures on the show and I could see Raghav – Tweedledee – was impressed.

'Let's move on to the second – live the celeb life for a day.' Before I could give any figures about it, a Punjabi guy called TJ interrupted me, saying, 'Wait a minute. I don't agree.' Then he went on to tell everyone that he'd overheard people talking positively about the first show, and everyone seemed to light up with this news. I was fuming. What did this fellow know? North Indians should just stay in the north drinking their RC. They are not refined, intellectual gentlemen like Bengalis, who only drink single malt. Superior taste means superior intelligence. A superior intelligence means the bloody fool was wrong and I was right.

'Just a minute TJ,' I said, cutting in, and then continued in a more calm manner, 'Just because you heard some canteen boys talking about the porn show doesn't mean the buyers have liked it. I have statistics on my side. Facts. Data. You want to say all that is nothing?'

'Not nothing OB, but you must take another viewpoint as well, shouldn't you?' he asked.

Others nodded their head in agreement and both Tweedledee and Tweedledum looked amused. They would rather have a fight take place in the conference than get any proper work done. It increased office politics and made for great gossip that would be circulated around for weeks. Kept most people occupied at lunch and around water coolers, instead of actual work getting done. Their shared belief was that fights showcased competitive spirit and passion in a corporate office. It also meant that their position was under no threat since the asses were busy fighting amongst themselves. Well played.

I didn't want to start a fight. But I was right. So I wanted to stand my ground. Who was this chit of a Royal Challenge whiskey drinker to say that I, me, Obrokranti Banerjee (who drank, or rather had drunk, once, in the Kolkata Club and thoroughly enjoyed and chosen to make it his drink, eighteen-year-old, extremely rare Glenmorangie) was wrong?

So I replied, 'Of course we are all free to take everyone's opinions, but the opinions that count are the advertisers', don't you think? If they don't give money for the program, then how can we run it? Or are you saying we should spend more money and do more research on this just to keep the program going? That would mean spending three lakh rupees an episode, TJ. Where will it come from? Shall we all go out with a donation box to collect it?'

For a moment, he may have considered it. The entire room was quiet, waiting for him to respond so they could take sides and scream 'Go TJ' or 'Go Obro' while we wrestled on the boardroom table.

'I just think we should try to rope in the sales people for this meeting and see if they can do an integration and keep this show alive.'

Tweedledee butted in, 'Why don't we have anyone from sales here? Didn't anyone call them? Don't they know how important these meetings are? TJ, make a note and tell them your idea when we get back. And next time they should join us for these brainstorming sessions.'

Another tactic to divert from work in a corporate office is to blame people. Who should have done what. And why wasn't so and so informed. It can take hours, at the end of which people are exhausted and need a break from talking about nothing important.

Even though I had won this round, TJ was from the land of makki ki roti and sarson da saag and wouldn't let anything go. He would argue this out or get revenge. Neither of which I was looking forward to. You see, I am a gentle type of a man. I would rather just read books and smoke a pipe while listening to music, and have someone press my feet and my wife bring me some tea and Marie biscuits. That's all I want from life. But to get there I need to work hard, keep my bosses happy and not make colleagues want to take revenge on me. This is too tough sometimes.

I continued to present the rest of the slides and thankfully a plate of biscuits soon came into the conference room and I gobbled down some twenty of them before the half-empty plate was passed around. My presentation took a little longer because of the delay caused by TJ and me fighting on almost every point, and it was almost three o'clock when we broke for lunch.

I was starving again by then, and filled my plate at the buffet counter just in case I couldn't get in line for seconds. I sat in one corner and my semi-friend Menon came by. I call him my semi-friend because we hang out in office sometimes and step out for smokes together. I know nothing about his life and he hasn't the faintest clue about mine. We just nod to each other and speak in monosyllables. Why can't all my relationships be this good?

He sat next to me and said, 'Hello.'

I looked up at him and said a cheerful, 'Hello.'

We ate in silence. A bearer came to ask us if we wanted something to drink and we both asked for a Coke. At that moment, this man was the only person in the world who was in sync with me. After we finished eating, someone cleared our plates, he offered me a cigarette, and I took it. We sat and smoked, looking around at a few people chattering away, the gossipy types who wanted to network. TJ was speaking to Ramesh – Tweedledum – trying to suck up to him even more. These Punjabis, I tell you; they'll try to make an impression any opportunity they get. I wanted to say something profound to Menon so I blew out smoke and said, 'Market deck next, huh?' He nodded. I nodded back. That was it. We got each other. *We* didn't need words. We didn't have dreams that needed explanation. There was an underlying communication that meant, 'I don't really care, but I'm here bro!' We finished smoking and went back inside the conference room.

TJ gave me a dirty look as he sat down. I ignored him. Gentlemen do not respond to such kind of behaviour. And I intend to be one. The rest of the session went off well – TJ butted in on most of the presentations, and by the end of it, both Tweedledee and Tweedledum told him to shut up so they could get on with it. I think they were both so bored they wanted the bar to open ASAP (as soon as possible).

We wrapped up at the dot of six. The poor marketing intern who was in the middle of saying something got cut off by Tweedledee, who announced, 'That's a wrap, guys. We have other important matters to discuss.'

Suddenly the bickering, accusatory, opinionated men became long-lost buddies willing to share anything in the world. They all headed to the bar with far better spirit and even ribbed each other about how they had been downloading the porn anchor show on their laptops. I looked at them and sighed. I had to head back to my lovely girlfriend who had already given me twenty-one missed calls and sent twelve text messages asking whether I had left or not.

As I got onto my bike, TJ and Menon walked out of the

bar with drinks in their hands. When they saw me, TJ burst out laughing so hard, he spilled half his drink. He must have already downed one or two shots of his RC inside. Menon, however, looked at me with an expression of sympathy, and with a half smile that only made his face look crooked, he raised his hand to say bye. He knew. He understood. I raised my hand too, and kept it there a second longer as if to say, 'May the force be with us.'

And with that, I called Radha to tell her I was on my way home, and yes, I was looking forward to meeting her after such a long time. It had only been twelve hours since I'd left the house. Women count the seconds while you're away. Men count the days to be away.

Radha makes me feel what the poor ring must have felt about Gollum. I am playing 'Radha and her "Precious" Obrokanti'.

4

As I headed back home from Madh island, I saw my life racing past in my mind. How had I ended up like this? At the tender age of twenty-eight, I was already moulded (AKA 'changed for the better') by my girlfriend, owned by my boss and whipped by my landlord. I could have easily stayed in Kolkata and lived in a palatial ancestral home with a large family that pampered me. Instead, I chose to leave it to pursue another dream. The dream of having more women than my stupid cousin Lengtu.

Lengtu is the complete opposite of me. He has a way with words. He can charm anyone and he has a dazzling smile that women think is genuine. Genuine my ass. All he has wanted from an early age is to get into their pants. He would get into our aunt's room – pretending that he'd forgotten the way to his room – just to watch her change her sari. When he was eleven, he saved up his allowance so he could buy binoculars to look into the neighbour's house where a teenage girl would change into her pyjamas at the dot of ten every night. He begged our father to give him a bike on his fifteenth birthday just so he could take the girls from school for a ride. And then parked in some dark spot to make out.

I was awkward. I tried his moves but they always backfired and soon I lost confidence. So I would tag along with him whenever I wanted to spend time with a woman. He would find two female friends then, and the one he didn't like would be mine for the evening. Obviously, I didn't do anything with her. I never knew what kind of conversation would lead up to a kiss. And what would make her sleep with me. My conversation starters were, 'So do you like Chandler from *Friends*? What is your favourite colour? Do you like chemistry or physics?'

Sometimes the woman would respond with some affirmation and we would chat about TV shows for a bit. Nothing sensuous. Nothing interesting. And then she would mysteriously get a headache and have to leave. It was no wonder that I was a virgin until I met Radha. I would just come home and masturbate like mad. I respected women, even though I didn't understand them. I couldn't use them like sex toys. What an idiot I was. So much time wasted. So many lost opportunities. When youth finally slipped away, and I found Radha, I held on to her as tightly as she held on to me. The one woman in my life who I could coax into giving me sex. And somewhere that's where the challenge lies. If a woman gives in easily, there's no fun. You need to use your masculine skills for her to finally say yes. Though, to do it every night is a bit tedious and sometimes you just want to tell her, 'I've run out of romantic things to say. Now please can you just take off your clothes?'

You would think that everyone gets to have sex in college. It's the freedom years man. Men should be bedding women like mad. But my mother loved me so much that even when I entered college, she would make sure she would drop me and pick me up. It was most embarrassing and it's probably the reason I never got laid in those three years.

Lengtu insisted on taking the bus and his mother let him. But my mother used to say that her sister was making the biggest mistake by doing so. I think she was over-protective about me. She said I was too precious to be sent in the bus. I couldn't blame her. I am an only child, while Lengtu has a younger sister, Nandini. Also, I am far better looking than Lengtu anyway. He is just tall. That's why he got the pet name (*daak naam*) Lengtu. My *bhaalo naam* (real name on tenth standard board exam papers) Obrokranti is as bad as my *daak naam* Paantha, which means castrated goat. Seriously. My friends gave me that name in college. Till then my mother called me Bablu.

All my Bengali friends have *daak naam*s: Potla, Hulo, Nadu, Habul, Ghoton, Gogol, Babush, Bubam, Bujum and Jadu for boys, and Tepi, Puchki, Tuni, Buni, Tumpa, Rinku, Khukhu, Munnie for girls. With some Facebook friend requests now, I have no idea who they are. I've never heard their real names.

Lengtu would tell me about his exploits with women from the first year of college itself. It started from the first Durga Puja in college where he asked a woman where he should stand in line for *pushpanjali*, since he wanted to thank Ma Durga for all the blessings in his life. Bull. He wanted to stand closer to the woman and look down her blouse. She was quite impressed and later showered him with blessings in the park behind the *pandal*. Bloody hell.

When I tried the same tactic the next day, the woman said in a loud voice so the entire *pandal* could hear, '*Oie deeke aache aar iktu shoro!*' (That side and move a little!) I was so embarrassed that I didn't even attend Maha Navami pujo, which is my favourite because of the awesome *bhog* we get later.

By the end of those five days of Durga Puja, Lengtu told me he had been with five women. I said the only thing that I had learnt in college that we used mercilessly to anyone who tried to bullshit us, '*Baler kotha* Basuram *ke giye bolo.*' Talk such bullshit to Basuram and not to me. (*Bal* – slang for pubic hair, used as figure of speech to denote inferior conversation.)

To trump Lengtu, I decided to do an MBA. It horrified everyone.

'Law *korbe na*?' shouted my grandmother. 'It's the best profession in the world and your Dadabhai said that if you have the gift of the gab and an intelligent mind, you can fool anyone in this world.'

Dadabhai had a brilliant mind. He was one of the best lawyers in the country. However, his progeny and their progeny neither had the gift of talking nor the brains to do anything worthwhile – according to my grandmother. Hence, they couldn't pass the law exam and instead went into soft fields like media, or chartered accountancy. She was still trying to convince at least one grandchild to take up law to continue the legacy, but none of us was interested in it, especially after watching *Jolly LLB*, the Bollywood film that showed how lawyers actually turn out. Because of course, Bollywood reflects the true reality of our times.

I told my family the world was moving towards MBAs and the degree would mean I would get more money into the house. I didn't tell them then my secret desire was to go to Mumbai. The land of voluptuous women who wouldn't have a problem if I stood close to them, because there is simply no space in Mumbai to stand at all anyway.

After my MBA, I got through an on-campus job in Mumbai. It would be in television, and I would start as a marketing associate. Television, I thought, was wonderful. All those women dressed in skimpy outfits not bothering how I was looking at them. It was then a 'lifestyle channel' that had bikini shoots on beaches, travel shows (with two women in bikinis for the most part), women getting on in spas and food shows (hopefully with women in bikinis making aloo poshto). What better place for me to be – my two desires fulfilled. And the pay didn't seem too bad for a twenty-five-year old.

So I jumped at the chance. There was hell when I told the family at home. My grandmother fainted in her typical dramatic style and my mother cried into her pallu. Lengtu had chosen to take his Civil Services exam, again. It was his third and final try. The ass had failed twice before and had taken an entire year to study for it. He was still considered the good boy of the house, because taking exams is considered noteworthy in my family whereas working in a menial position and earning to support yourself is beneath them.

Lengtu barely cared what he did in life as long as he did many women. He used studying as an excuse to join several classes where he would meet different women.

I was the bad sperm that had decided to leave Kolkata and join, of all things, something as disreputable as the media industry. But I promised my mom that I would call four times a day and I would visit every Durga Puja. I told her I would send money back home so she could buy pretty things, and that she could stay with me whenever she wanted to get away from Thakuma, my grandmother. That helped a bit since she has never got along with her mother-in-law. I tried to speak to my father but he said I could do what I wanted, and went back to reading his Dostoevsky. He is the best father in the world.

The channel put me up in a guesthouse for a month till I found my own place. I thought I would manage something close to the office so I wouldn't have to commute so much. That way I would have more time to try and meet girls. This was the first time I had triumphed over Lengtu. I told him when I was packing to leave, 'I'm going to find hotter, bustier women in Mumbai who will lust after me, and you will still have the same Bengalis here. Haha Lengtu da. Who's the smarter one now?'

He was silent, knowing I had beaten him for now. But he smiled and said, 'All the best bro. You'll finally lose it.'

And I did. With Radha. The One and the Only. Who was waiting for me at home. There had better be some food when I got back, I thought. I was starving and craving fish. I needed energy to sleep with her tonight. If I was going back all the way without having a single drink and a single karaoke song, she had better be lying naked in bed for me. The least she could do.

Great insight – women want us to change into better people. Though they rarely remain the same from the time we meet them!

5

When I got home I saw that Radha was sitting in a corner going through my box of condoms. Yes, I have a box of them on my side table. It looked like she was pricking holes in them. This was not a good sign.

Thank God I always carry a spare in my wallet. I've been carrying one in case I get lucky at a bar. That has not happened yet, but a man should be ready at all times. As the nincompoop CEO says all the bloody time, 'Luck is nothing but opportunity meeting preparation.' And claims that it's his original line, though everyone knows it was Baba Ramdev.

As soon as Radha saw me, she quickly closed the box and ran to me. 'You're home,' she said while flinging her arms around me. Her boobs felt so good against my chest. After a long day staring at ugly men, it was actually nice to come home to a loving woman with large breasts. That was a very good quality about her. I had triumphed over Lengtu in at least that category. He had been dating a girl for the last few months who was small-chested. He was afraid that if it lead to marriage, he would never hold big boobs in his hands again. He was thinking it was time to bring up the *kundli*, and in the process 'get some space', but she had refused to give him her date, time and place of birth. Haha. She was clever, and now Lengtu was stuck!

I started kissing Radha, but she was not ready. Women never are! I mean, for all the *Cosmo* magazines they subscribe to, they should at least try some of the moves suggested. Like get naked to begin with. Even for that men have to say, 'Baby, please let me take off your shirt.' And they'll reply, 'No. In a bit. Let's kiss first.' Just do it woman! Even after a hard day's work and driving for several hours, women's ridiculous problems like not having internet at home will be too stressful for them to take off their clothes quietly or give you a blow job. Bloody rubbish.

I had to do all the foreplay and every bit of nonsense that it required to get her in the mood. Earlier I used to just kiss her and she was ready. Now it took forever. And I was afraid I would lose my erection if I had to do any more necking. The time taken to have an orgasm is inversely proportional to the time taken to beg the woman to be ready. So I finished rather quickly and Radha hadn't. Too bad. If I couldn't drink with the boys, I wasn't going to give her any pleasure either.

I put on the TV and asked what was for dinner. Radha said that the maid had made some chicken curry and roti.

'Again?' I whined. 'Every day we have chicken curry and roti. Or dal makhani. Or aloo paratha. It's just too much, I say. Just because you want everything Punjabi doesn't mean I do. I want to have fish. I want to have poshto. I want to have bhaja,' I said, sounding like a five-year-old child. I missed my mommy.

Radha came over, cuddled with me, switched the channel to Zee Café and said, 'You know I don't like the smell of mustard oil. And I can't stand fish. Why can't you be a little more adjusting?'

I took the remote from her, changed the channel back to where the Bengali war hero Arnab Goswami was ranting and said, 'Okay give me whatever there is. I'm tired.' And then I put my feet up while she went to heat up the food. The things I do for her. Give her sex. Not eat fish. Too much for a true-blooded Bengal tiger like me. One of these days I'm going to snap.

While she was inside, I began to think about how we had met. After a year of moving to Mumbai, I realized that I wasn't getting anywhere with the women in office, and it wasn't easy to meet girls in the cheap drinking joints I went to with my colleagues. And we could only afford cheap drinking joints. My salary actually came to nothing much once they took away PF, gratuity, taxes, LTA, and other shit that the government loots us of. I was left with some seventeen thousand rupees in hand. With that budget, I couldn't find a place close to my office. I finally moved into a one-bedroom place in IC Colony, Borivali. I shared it with a roommate, a nice south Indian boy in my office, but in sales. He travelled often and I had the place to myself most days. This suited me well. We became thick friends, ate at the local Banjara restaurant almost every night, and travelled to work together in the local train. We didn't have much of a life, but we used to drink practically every night and it made us as thick as the tyre around middle-aged Bengali men.

But we never found women. The women who came to these joints had a rate and we preferred alcohol to a suspicious-looking thing in a short red skirt with hairy legs. After all, we had some dignity. I wasn't Lengtu!

I have an aunt in Mumbai called Shoma mashi. She is the oldest of my mother's sisters. My mother has six sisters scattered across the world. Clearly my grandfather had been very busy. Anyway, this Mumbai sister visited us in Kolkata once or twice and pulled my cheeks even when I was twenty-one years old. I had tried to avoid her like the plague after that. One day, out of the blue, she called me and said my mother had given her my number to check up on me. One of the reasons I had come to Mumbai was to get away from my Bengali clan, but it seemed to be chasing me even here. Anyway, no matter which part of the world you go, there will always be a Bengali there. And if you start chatting with them, you'll realize that you're somehow related. And if nothing else, we are all descendants of Rabindranath Tagore and hence need to bond.

'*Tumi bhalo acho*? Phone *kano korle na*?' (Are you well? Why didn't you call?), she asked, as if it were my one-point program to call or meet her. I gave some excuse but then she invited me for her grandson's first birthday party. 'It's going to be a grand affair at my house in Kandivali. You *have* to come. You live so close by. I don't want to hear any excuses. I'm sending you an SMS with my address. Saturday, four o'clock onwards.'

'Living close by' means nothing in Mumbai. It will still take you two hours to reach a place that is two kilometres away. Either there is a procession, some digging, or a visarjan or a wedding or a protest that will cause traffic to crawl. The entire chawl is on the streets and every policeman unavailable to clear the path for your smooth movement. Every Mumbaikar says, 'On a good day I can reach the place in twenty minutes.' This good day never comes, and it generally takes between one to three hours to reach anywhere. The good day must have happened when the final over of an India-Pakistan cricket match was on and the entire country was watching TV while you and some chutiya were trying to see if you could reach the place in twenty minutes.

Living close by could also mean you are neighbours. Like right across the corridor. A place that would take you two steps to reach. But even then, if you're next door neighbours, you rarely meet. Mumbaikars may be friendly but they definitely don't want to be your friends. They have their own thick group that they rarely meet. Unless you're Gujju, which is a whole different story. Then you would meet for breakfast, lunch, dinner, coffee, anniversaries, birthdays, cards parties, movies, and still take vacations together because you feel you haven't met each other enough.

If you're not Gujju, you probably never have the time or the inclination to see your relatives. And even if you do have the time and inclination, the feeling passes quite quickly and you decide you would rather watch TV. Even in this digital era of Whatsapp, BBM and text messaging, who really wants to know how their relatives are doing? That's what conversations with your mother on Sundays are for. So she can fill you in while you pretend to listen.

I tried to give Mashi some excuse for not coming. I said I had work but she said everyone in Mumbai is working and not to give her such gyaan. Then I said, 'I'm quite broke, Mashi. I don't know what to get Babush.'

'*Ei kee*! Such formality! Just come. Otherwise I'll tell your mother that you still haven't visited me.'

At the thought of my mother giving me a long lecture, I ran out of what to say. These are the times when I feel my super-brain should be working, but after dealing with bad programming people all day, even I run out of excuses. So I agreed to go for her grandson's birthday party.

Living in Mumbai can get lonely. Besides work and your roommate, you don't have anyone else unless you get into a group. And most groups are couple centric. It's the wives who socialize and get their men to meet so a group is formed. Antisocial guys like me don't know how to make friends or get into groups. Actually, most men just go to work and come home to empty apartments. They don't know how to meet and talk to women, and their Friday nights are spent watching TV / porn at home or playing on their PlayStation till dawn. Rarely do they realize they're lonely. Except when they're horny or drunk and really want a woman in their lives.

When I got to the birthday party, the only person who seemed out of place was Radha. She was not a mother who had brought a child, or a grandmother sitting and being served by servants, or any of the uncles who were smoking on the balcony or a maid running after a child. She was a distant cousin of someone who was at the party. No one knew why she was there. She probably didn't either. When I first noticed her, she was standing in the balcony, alone. She looked lovely, her long brown hair cascading down over her huge bosom. Later I would only remember that she was wearing something that showed off her cleavage. Hence, we instantly connected. I used my line and then asked, 'You wanna be my girlfriend?' And she laughed, thought it was so cute and said, 'Yes!' I should have recognized that as a psycho sign. I did not. She sure had me at hello.

She wooed me. I thought that was very hot. A woman wanting me. A big-breasted woman desiring me. But obviously God had saved the best part for later. She took my number and called me repeatedly when I was in office. I would tell her when I was leaving for home, and she would take a rickshaw to my place. Then we would make mad passionate love and fall asleep. I remember I called Shubir immediately after I had lost my virginity to her. 'Lengtu, I did it,' I said in utter jubilation. And he sleepily said, '*Baler kotha Basuram ke giye bolo.*' (Tell such bullshit to someone else.) Bastard didn't believe me. So I went back to bed and did it another time just to prove to him that I could. And told him the next morning again. This time he was impressed. Finally.

Soon Radha moved in and, before I knew it, she was asking when I was coming home after work on a daily basis. She had parents and a large family who were settled in Pune, and she was a typical Punjabi kudi. She was strong, aggressive and wild in bed. She managed my household affairs and I was most relieved that I didn't have to do any of those women chores anymore. You know, like order food, or washing underwear. Now Radha would instruct the bai to do it.

One day I came home and remembered I had a roommate who lived with me. I asked her about him, 'Has Ravi gone for another shoot?' She looked at me and said, 'Who's Ravi?' I was bewildered. I had introduced them, I think, once upon a time, so I said, 'My roommate.' She shook her head and dismissed it as if I were mad: 'You didn't have one.' I went to check his cupboard and it was filled with her clothes. Her toiletries lay all around the bathroom, and many food items that I never ate were stacked neatly in the kitchen cabinets. Like fruits, digestive biscuits and Baked Lays Chips. Who the fuck eats baked potato chips?

I mumbled to myself, 'I never had so much food in the house. We always ate at Banjara.'

After a while, when I was less stoned, I pried it out of Radha. She said one day a guy had come in and eaten the food she had asked the cook to make. She had been most upset and he had left after that. Later I found out from people in my office that she had thrown all his clothes out of the window because, when she had returned after a parlour visit, he had been rearranging her things. My poor roommate also quit his sales job around the same time. Probably because he didn't have any clothes. Since then we have lost touch.

Two years have passed like this, and here I am, pandering to every need of Radha's and unable to figure out if this is a good life or not. My pay has gone from five to eight lakh, but still there is nothing in hand. It is as if the carrot is perpetually in front of my eyes but I never get it. Further taxes have hit and the same amount comes in hand every month. I could barely get by on my own, and now I have been supporting Radha as well. Honestly, I wonder what would have happened if I hadn't gone up to her at the party. Or if Mashi had not called that day. Or if my super-brain had actually worked and come up with a good excuse. Or if I hadn't moved to Mumbai at all.

Maybe I would still be a virgin. Now that's a scary thought.

6

Was sitting at home after a wonderful session where Radha had agreed to graze my balls with her fingers. It was truly magical for the five seconds it lasted. Women rarely do anything to make you happy sexually. And when they do, it's for such a short time that you feel so grateful. Then they'll milk it for as long as they can, as if they've done you the biggest favour on the planet. You didn't bail me out of jail, woman. You just made me cum. Which I did myself anyway. But fine, I'll take you shopping. Whatever.

My reverie was broken with a Whatsapp message. It was Nandini, my cousin from Kolkata, asking how the conference had gone. I was chatting with her when Radha walked out of the kitchen. She looked suspiciously at my phone, and at my smile, and decided to ruin my mood. 'Who are you talking to?' she asked.

'Nandini,' I replied.

The ever-so-calm woman burst out, 'WHO THE FUCK IS SHE? ARE YOU CHEATING ON ME?'

So here's a thing I've learnt in this relationship. When a woman is freaking out, the idea is to not dismiss her. You cannot say, like I did, 'Oh, please.' Also, do not roll your eyes while voicing the above statement. This could lead to some injury.

She punched me hard on my arm and shouted some more, 'What do you mean, "*Oh please*"? Do my feelings not count? You're not denying you're having an affair!'

I tried to calm her down. 'Radha. Nandini is my *cousin*. We are very close. She's like my sister. We grew up together.'

But she would have none of it. She said this rakhi/cousin sister stuff was ridiculous; only an actual blood sister was fine. One could easily screw a rakhi sister. There was no law that said you couldn't. I tried to pacify Radha, but she had a fit, claiming that she had given up her life to spend time with me, and was away from her entire family so she could look after me, and here I was having phone sex with a so-called cousin!

I told her that I would take her out for a lovely ride on my Yamaha bike. I had made that one investment so I wouldn't have to walk in the muck of a Mumbai monsoon to the train station. She calmed down, we ate dinner, and then I took her for a long ride to have ice-cream. She felt much better after that and I thought the matter had been dropped.

The next morning I saw that all my conversations had been deleted on my phone and my Whatsapp obliterated completely. She had also deleted every girl's number, except my mother's. I dared not question her. I didn't want an outburst again. I decided I would feed in Nandini's number later under a male Bengali name. Radha would never suspect I was talking to a girl if her alias was Debobroto.

Little did I realize that she would only get more suspicious and paranoid later. (Great insight: Women never forget things. They only have temporary amnesia when you gift them something after a fight.)

. In order to help my fellow hapless souls, I now present you with a guide, which I have prepared after intense hours of studying the internet. May it help you. If not, there is always 'Naughty America'.

Five Ways to Get Your Girlfriend to Have Sex

1. Romance her. Flowers, candles, food. The three pillars that will make your pillar have an all-nighter. But if you can't go to such lengths, put on her favourite songs and start dancing with her. Do not grind! Keep your crotch away from her lady parts while dancing. Mumble, 'Your hair smells really nice.' A nice compliment will always get you in bed.

2. Give her presents. Buying something nice for her will always be appreciated with sex. If you've gone shopping with her and let her pick something out, you're the dream man who's getting laid tonight!

3. Talk about the future. Tell her how lovely it will be when you get married and go on a honeymoon. Switzerland. Cottages. Fireplaces. Molten chocolate. Satin sheets. Say all the things women have read about in those damn Mills & Boons novels. Painting a picture gets their juices flowing.

4. Balance sensitivity. Ask about her day (but not in any way that will have her give you details). Asking something personal always makes a woman want to open up to you in more ways than one. Gently start massaging her shoulders to ease her tension. Don't run it hard for two minutes and ask her to take her clothes off. Say encouraging things. Get her a glass of water or a drink. Make sure she's relaxed and comfortable. Not enough to actually start chatting with you, but enough for her to 'take her mind off things' by having

sex. Play with her hair, run your fingers gently down the side of her neck. DO NOT go near her breasts. Kiss her softly on her neck, back, lips. Leave out any zone that you really want to touch. Pull back after kissing her passionately. Look into her eyes deeply and let her go. Allow her then to take the initiative.

5. Be confident. When it's a first time, women will have walls. Speak confidently about it and move through the hurdles. 'I don't even know you.' Reply, 'Yes you do. It's me.' 'We're moving too fast.' Reply, 'I think the speed is just right. Or are you just faking that smile?' Say it with a sexy and confident smile. You'll have her in no time! Do not burp or fart at any point. Make sure you eat light before the seduction. You can't use the same tactics every night. Change your game and pretty soon you'll be doing it at least twice a week!

7

By the time Monday came around, I was most happy to get back to work. That's because the ideal weekend, which involves lazing in bed, watching cricket and Govinda movies, was converted by my clingy girlfriend into a fight fest over my Facebook friends.

By Sunday morning, Radha had scoured through my laptop, all documents, files, excel sheets; she even went online and onto my Facebook page. Then all hell broke loose. She scrutinized each and every girl's profile and sent them a message from my account, calling them dirty whores.

No wonder I got a message on my phone from a distant cousin calling me a 'fat bastard'. I was quite taken aback until I realized what she had done. When I tried to log into my Facebook account later, I realized the password had been changed.

'Why do you even need to connect with your old girlfriends?' she asked. When I tried to reason that most of the 'girls' were either cousins, aunts or colleagues, there was a huge uproar. 'I DON'T fucking care,' was her simple explanation. I obviously tried to use *her* FB account as an analogy, to which she said, 'You can access my account

whenever you want. There is no hanky-panky there.'
Implication, accusation, judgement and guilt pronounced in
such rapid succession is an art Radha has doctored in. She
then wanted to know all my passwords and suggested we
have a 'common password' to both our accounts. I quickly
pretended to have an intense bowel movement and headed
to the bathroom. But she continued to insist, even following
me inside. I could only relent and say, 'Well then keep our
passwords as Radha-I-love-you-please-don't-harass-me.'

She stared at me and finally said, 'Okay. I'm sorry. As long
as you're honest with me I won't get upset. But as soon as
you start hiding things, it annoys me. Just be truthful and I'll
be all right.' She said this in her sweetest tone, and I was
shocked. Radha was behaving most out of character. I knew
something was up. Later when I checked my laptop, she had
not only set a picture of us together as the wallpaper, but
sent the same photograph out in a mail to 'everyone' on my
address list with the subject: 'I'm engaged !'

On Monday, therefore, everyone in office began
congratulating me. I denied it, telling everyone that women
blow things out of proportion, but obviously people thought
it was really strange. I was also mad at Radha because the
picture she chose had been taken when we travelled to Goa a
few months ago and I was half-naked. With my hairy chest
and a bit of pot belly showing, my stupid colleagues couldn't
stop grinning ear to ear. Damn Radha. Couldn't she have
found a better picture? Or better yet, not sent out a mail. Or
better yet, not gone through my laptop?

But the weekend hadn't ended there. Instead of letting
me sit on the couch and watch the Test series, Radha insisted
we watch the latest Shah Rukh Khan movie. Because she

adored him and thought he was the king of romance. I knew this would end badly for me. I was the king of gas. There would be many comparisons in the movie and by the end I would want to throttle SRK's neck for a shoddy movie (he always made movies I couldn't connect to – no, not even *Chak De*, because even there he didn't have gas), and giving women false hopes about men and relationships. If there were a petition to ban his movies, I would definitely sign it. If there were a ban on damn romantic novels I would sign that too. And I would definitely sign a petition to make porn and marijuana legal. The best fuckin' combination since maach-bhaat.

Shah Rukh owned Kolkata Knight Riders and therefore, considering my Bengali roots, I should be a fan. But it wasn't so. He was arrogant, charming, friendly, and intelligent, and therefore nothing like the goofs he played on screen. I would happily watch an SRK docu-series (which came out like clockwork, once every two years), but I thought nothing on earth could compel me to watch the latest SRK tear fest. There I was though, watching an SRK film because I wanted to be the perfect boyfriend for Radha. SRK can continue to be a girl's dream man, but he definitely wasn't a man's man.

I was in seat H6, and watching the last of the movies directed by Yash Chopra (Yash uncle to Radha as well). The movie, as predicted, was lousy. Radha loved it. It was a hundred and eighty minutes long, and all I could think of at the end of it was how sore my ass felt. '*Jab tak hai gaand*,' I said to Radha. She was not amused.

The only good thing about it was that Radha let me eat everything on the snacks tray. I gorged on oily two-day-old samosas, cheese popcorn, a large coke, a chicken burger and tea, all the things that she said were unhealthy and wouldn't allow me to have usually. Yes, Radha had put me on a diet.

Word of advice – DO NOT put Bengali men on a diet. They get cranky. They need food. It's the only good thing in their lives.

But Radha had said I needed to lose weight and started giving me salad, roti, boiled chicken and vegetables. Of course my body started protesting. This was not food. Food for a Bengali means something that satisfies his soul. Not just fills his stomach. It can be healthy as long as it's tasty. The problem is, I've rarely seen anything in Indian cuisine that is tasty *and* healthy. Continental, yes. But then, no bai knows how to make roast duck with mushroom sauce. To add to the misery, she even stopped putting a sweet dish in the *dabba*. A *mishti* is most important at the end of the meal. And a *paan*. But a *paan* can be skipped, if there is nothing around. But a *mishti* after lunch and dinner makes a meal complete. There is no other way to look at it. So I resorted to buying a bowl of curd at the canteen, adding four teaspoons of sugar in it, and eating it as a sweet dish. Any Bengali can have doi-cheeni at any time. But it still wasn't the same as a sandesh, roshogulla, or even a bar of chocolate.

Finally, instead of eating her packed dabba every day, I started going out for lunch and gave my dabba to the canteen boy to eat. It was a perfect set-up. Radha didn't know what was happening because an empty tiffin box came home five days a week.

All this had gone on for a full two months, until last Thursday.

Radha had given me lauki sabzi, dal, curd and two rotis. That is not food for a man. It's food for a dog. Bloody hell.

Was she just trying to piss me off? I had already had a terrible morning, with my boss yelling at me for no apparent reason, and now I had to eat this shit. I wanted to let off steam. I wanted to feel good about myself. I needed a good hearty meal with starch, meat, and oil. I gave my tiffin to the canteen boy and told him if he didn't want it to give it to the cow behind the office as a good gesture. Then I proceeded with a few colleagues to the nearest restaurant to order some real food.

Things were going so well. We got our appetizers of chicken tikkas and mutton rolls and I was already feeling slightly better. Then the main course came – rice, chicken gravy, fish fry, mutton sukha and paratha. I dug in with gusto.

Now, when boys eat, there is absolute silence at the table. No one wants to talk or share what their day has been like. We do not pick at our food like women, with the hope that we don't look like gluttons while eating. In fact, when boys eat, it looks like the feast at the end of every Asterix comic, where there is food flying all over the place, dirty hands, stained shirts, silly grins, and loud voices demanding waiters to bring them more food. That's a meal.

Amidst all this laughter and noisy eating, I was just about to put a handful of fish and rice in my mouth, when I saw her. Radha. Standing at the door.

In such a situation, a man would rather just finish his meal than make a run for it. I saw Radha walk towards me in slow motion – like the slow motion run that women did in all SRK movies, with him standing with his arms wide open to let them know they needed a point to stop at – and my balls split wide open. Instead of stepping back from the food and making a run for it, my super-brain decided that this could be the last meal I would have and I quickly gobbled up some four-five large bites of food before she got to the table. I finally looked up at her and she was glaring down at me.

My colleagues didn't even glance at us. Bastards were too busy eating to notice if one of their own was getting murdered. I could see the fumes coming out of Radha's ears. I quietly licked my fingers, walked to the wash basin to wash my hands and followed her outside the restaurant. Only then did one colleague raise his head. 'Eh, at least give money for your portion, bastard,' he said. Asshole. Didn't he see that I hadn't even made out a will yet, and this would be the last meal of my life? But since I had no Facebook friends left, I thought it would be wise to at least have a few colleagues on my side. So I put a few hundred buck notes on the table and left.

Radha gave it to me. In full force. She asked me how often I came here, what food I ate and who were the morons who encouraged this behaviour. She then went on to tell me how unhealthy it was, and that I didn't love her. What has my eating got to do with my love for her? She explained that she packed a dabba for me with great love and care. *Ghanta*. She told the cook what to make while she sat on her pretty ass reading the papers every morning before I left.

She also said she wanted to see me look lean and fit like Shah Rukh Khan. That man, I tell you, I can hate him in so many ways. And she went on to explain that, because I was getting so heavy, she was feeling crushed under my weight in bed. What? I had not gained *that* much weight. And I barely pressed down on her. Didn't she know sex was an art that all men had perfected since birth? No man puts his whole body weight down on a woman. If we did that, then they would see how strong we are. We propped ourselves up on our elbows and did most of the work while they enjoyed it. Weight was not an issue there. But trust Radha to make it about that. And since that was the only thing that connected us, I promised to get back on my diet and said I would never cheat on it again. Yes I did. Because that's what you do when you want to stop women from crying. Otherwise the waterworks just don't bloody end.

I went back to office where the boys were having a burping competition, but since I had swallowed my pride, I went back to my desktop quietly and swore to take revenge one day.

Great insight: If women are losing an argument, they'll start crying. The waterworks does a man in. We give in every time.

8

I woke up again with a hard on. I'd been dreaming of Sunny Leone in the new video I downloaded. I'd watched it in office yesterday and had been thinking about it all night long. It had been a few weeks since the conference. The jokes in office about my leaving early, being hairy, and engaged, had finally died down by Friday. But I had shown them. I had got past a firewall in the wretched admin server and downloaded a video on my computer. I had quickly erased all trace of it as well, but the small joy I had by accomplishing this was enough.

I turned to my side and opened my eyes. Radha was sitting up and staring at me. What the...

She smiled sweetly and asked, 'What are you leaving me in your will?'

I closed my eyes again. I hoped this was a bad dream. I opened my eyes again and she had now propped herself nearer to me, one arm under her head and sheer determination in her face to figure out how many family jewels I would be leaving her.

'Shona,' I said as calmly as I could in my morning groggy voice of reason, using an endearing Bengali term to soften it, 'we're not even married yet.'

Slowly, very slowly, her smile turned into a scowl, and I could see my hard-on already whimpering away to its smallest size. Damn. Wrong answer. I should have said 'everything', and then at least had some sex.

She sat up, folded her arms and asked, 'And why aren't we married yet?'

Bokkachod Obro, now you've done it, said the little voice in my head.

I needed time to figure out how to respond. I decided to go to the bathroom to gather my thoughts, but when I got up from bed, she shrieked, 'Where are you going?'

I turned and said, 'To crap. Can I?'

She nodded quietly and I locked myself in the bathroom. I thought about marriage while sitting on the throne. I knew I wasn't ready. It's not as if I was commitment phobic. I mean I had stuck around with Radha for two years. And I had been completely faithful. But the basic difference between men and women is that women grow up thinking about what their wedding day will be like. Men never think about a wedding or marriage till they are actually sitting at the mandap.

Besides the fact that I wasn't ready, I knew that the family would want Nandini to get married first. She was twenty-five and if I plopped in there first with Radha and upset everyone's plans, God knows how they would react. I hadn't even explained my relationship with Radha to my family. My mother definitely had to meet her and approve of her for us to get married. I could not go against the family system. Hell, I would be left without an inheritance and with the way I was going in this flop channel, I would probably be fifty by the time I could get out of this apartment or buy a car.

And what about the other women? If I stuck to this woman all my life, I would never have a chance to sleep with the many women out there. This marriage business sounded all wrong. But I had to be shrewd. My super-brain had to come up with something to make her stay for now, but postpone this marriage topic for another time.

When I emerged from the bathroom, Radha was in the kitchen making breakfast – my favourite too: eggs and toast with lots of butter. Yum. Maybe she had forgotten the topic. She served me as I sat down at the tiny dining table with the newspaper.

'Here. Just the way you like your eggs – scrambled,' she said and placed my breakfast in front of me. I tried to be polite, like my mother had taught me, and asked, 'Where is your breakfast?'

She shook her head and said, 'I don't want any.'

I made the mistake of inquiring, 'Why?'

She replied, 'I like my eggs fertilized.'

I went back to reading the newspaper and eating my breakfast. There was no pleasing this woman. Ever since I had replaced the condom box and begun locking it, she had been sulking. My father had taught me how to deal with women: be sweet enough when you want sex, ignore when you don't want to answer a question, and sound irritated when nagged. So when Radha mentioned that she wanted to take me trousseau shopping this weekend, I looked deeper into my paper and grunted in annoyance. Unfortunately, Radha is not Bengali. She doesn't understand the nuances of a Bengali relationship. When a man grunts for more than a second, it means, 'Leave me alone.' Radha probably understood it as, '*Koi gal nahin. Suna nahin hoga.*' Ooff. Punjabis. Not intellectual at all. *Ki bolbo.*

I was saved by the bell when the cleaning maid arrived and Radha went to supervise. Mercifully, she would be busy and I could sit on the couch, in front of the TV, and fart in peace. A man needs to have space to pass gas. When we say, give us our space, that's what we mean. We want to sit alone somewhere in front of the TV and emit as much gas as we can without being judged. And with a woman in our daily life, it just becomes difficult to do so. Small pleasures become a chore. We give up so many things when we get married, including our freedom to sleep with whomever we want. I wasn't ready to give up my gas space just yet.

Since it was Saturday, I decided I would sit at home the whole weekend, without shaving, bathing or doing any work. Thankfully I didn't have a presentation to make on Monday morning, so I could enjoy the India–England Test series the entire weekend. After a long time I was going to relax and enjoy myself.

The maid cooked, cleaned and left quite quickly. She was efficient and listened to Radha diligently. Radha loved her and they worked well as a team. Maybe Radha could marry the maid, I thought, chuckling to myself. Only two hours to go before the match would start. I surfed channels and landed on an old movie with my favourite actor Mithun Chakraborty. It was somewhere in the middle, but I knew every frame of *Ek Aur Sikander*. This would be a good way to kill time till the match started. Then I could pass another eight hours. What an amazing weekend this would be.

Radha walked in and said, 'What are you watching?' I quickly reacted and hid the remote under my ass. I didn't want her to change the channel to some rubbish nonsense of a *saas-bahu* saga. I mean, that damn Anandi should die already.

The amount she cries on that soap *Uttaran*, man. Shit. I can't believe I even know those names. What am I becoming?

'Baby, you must watch this. It's hilarious. These old ham movies will make you laugh,' I said, opening my arms so she could snuggle up next to me, her big boobs resting on my chest. She came, sat and got bored rather quickly. Then I had another idea. I slid my hand under her Elco market nightie and cupped her breasts. I mean it takes tremendous imagination for a man to even want to do that. Get some slutty lingerie already. But this was a movement I had perfected over the last two years, ever since she had started wearing these ugly, dark, printed kaftans that she claimed were comfortable, but I thought made her look like a sack of potatoes. Nevertheless, undaunted by the woman in front of me, I whipped up an image in my head and found my way to her back and snapped open her bra with just two fingers. If only such things were appreciated on a CV in an interview, I would be head of the frickin' channel instead of assistant marketing manager.

Radha allowed me to feel her up a bit and just when I was getting into a happy space she asked, 'So when are we getting married?'

Ki bolbo! Women are such a pain in the ass. My mood went off immediately but it took all my willpower to hold on to the hard on, 'Radha let's talk about it as soon as I finish,' I said kissing her passionately. She complied. I made her get on top of me, then on the side, then I finally got on top of her and said, 'Now let me show you what a real man is made of.' And she moaned so loudly that Sunny would have been envious. Although when I looked at her for a brief second while I was cumming, Radha was gazing away as if she were bored. To be honest, I didn't care if she was faking it. If she was present, I didn't need to! And her breasts were magnificent.

I remembered how Lengtu and I would sit for hours discussing women's tits. We both prayed for a woman who was naturally 'gifted', and only one of us had been granted this wish.

I rolled off and went to the bathroom to light a cigarette. By now, she had guessed I smoked occasionally, but she didn't want it to stink up the apartment. Although it was my apartment that she had moved into, I dared not say that to her. When I came out and retook my old position on the couch, Radha went in for a shower, changed, came out and wanted to snuggle again. But this time I didn't have the patience. Leave a man be, *na*. I just gave you a good time.

The film had just got to the best part in the climax when Radha found the remote and switched it off.

'Now can we talk about our marriage?' she said with a raised eyebrow.

Crap. Women are like elephants. They never forget. And they'll always think they rule the jungle when actually the male alpha lion does. So I sat with Radha for the next four hours, missing the end of the film, skipping half the match commentary just to discuss our wedding plans.

Instead of actually committing to getting married, my super-brain came up with a plan on how to circumvent the topic – I asked her what kind of wedding she would like. So she went on to explain in great length the different functions she wanted, what she was going to wear, who we should invite, where we would stay. Blah blah blah. But I could pretend to be interested while watching the match in mute at least. By the time she was done, she was in such a happy mood that she forgot to ask if I even wanted to propose to her. She just assumed we would get married. I left it at that. Who wants to get into the nitty-gritty details? Let the woman be happy. It's a rare event anyway. At least she's off your case. And then she let me watch the remainder of the match in peace while she fiddled away on my laptop making lists for the wedding.

I had already learnt my lesson about letting her work on my laptop. This time I had password protected my porn collection and labelled it 'Data Analysis'. Also, the Twitter account I'd started to follow Sunny Leone had an egg as a display picture. I thought it was a great start to being secretive.

Here is one more guide. This is after intense meetings with the pros. Pros who are professionals at getting out of a marriage.

Five Ways to Get out of Discussing Marriage

1. Fake sickness. One can't do this too often, otherwise it'll become like the boy who cried wolf. But for the first three or four time, get an epileptic fit, rub ice on your palms and head and claim that you're feeling very ill. The woman will get into the looking-after-you mode and drop discussing marriage plans immediately.

2. Distract her. Bring up her childhood, talk about her work, ask about a parent's health, or the bai situation at home. Women can always start talking about something else. They just need someone who will listen to them and here's your opportunity to listen intently about everything under the sun except when you're getting married.

3. Compliment her. Tell her how beautiful she is and how eighty-five per cent of women put on at least five kilos after marriage, if not more. And then their beauty is lost. Forever. Let them start thinking about that. No woman wants to become fat.

4. Gossip. Ask her what happened to someone she knows who she doesn't speak to anymore. She'll start about that woman and won't stop. If she pauses, ask her about someone else – a childhood friend, a colleague, a girl in the building. Anyone. Women love to gossip and hopefully she'll get off the topic.

5. 'Hypothetically speaking'. Give them a hypothetical situation – what if you found someone you were attracted to, what would you do? What if we ran out of all our money, how would we survive? If we won the lottery, what would you want to do with it? Women can day dream for hours. Keep giving those ideas till they're in their own world and have completely forgotten about asking when you'll be getting married!

(Great insight: No matter how many times you watch *Gunda*, you'll always discover new nuggets. Kanti Shah is the God of all things.)

9

Women find the most inopportune time to pick a fight. For instance, right when you're in the middle of making a two hundred-slide presentation to impress your boss, who has given you the responsibility after eleven weeks of you asking for an 'opportunity to grow', and who will sign off on your KRAs because of this one particular project. If there were a national sport on how to annoy your boyfriend, Indian women would definitely win a gold medal.

The previous evening, Radha and I had had a fight. It was about some hypothetical situation. I had wondered, stupidly aloud, while watching Arnab Goswami scream at someone, if I got a job in Dubai, how much I would get paid. The little fantasy lasted for exactly five seconds before Radha burst it by saying, 'We can't move to Dubai. I don't want to leave India.' Now this got my goat. I did everything she said, so why wouldn't she want to do this for me? 'All my brothers are here,' she said. 'I can't leave my family to go to a foreign country. I'll be treated like a foreigner.'

As if she were being treated any better in Mumbai. Lately I had started understanding some Marathi words. I had heard it being used by some colleagues every time I passed their desks. I was no longer friends with them. The same words were used by our Maharashtrian maid, who cursed this Punjabi woman under her breath. Even she was getting fed up of Radha making her clean the house meticulously every day. No maid does it. They just want to take their *pagaar* and go on vacation.

So I told her, 'There's so much money to be made in Dubai. I can go and you can stay here. You can spend as much time with your brothers as you want then.'

The topic was closed for me, and I went back to watching Arnab, the one hour I could feel good watching a fellow Bengali scream at people older and more powerful than him. Something I dreamed of doing with Tweedledee and Tweedledum one day.

Obviously it was the wrong thing to say. She took the remote, switched off the TV and demanded that I 'rethink *carefully*' what I had just said. How I could even think of leaving her behind, she demanded.

'You can come and visit,' I suggested, rationally.

She shook her head. 'You can't go. That's final.'

Now who the hell was she to decide my future? I was the one who broke away from a strong Bengali household to come to Mumbai and pave my own path. And Radha wasn't even my wife. How could she just say *that's final*, and think I would be okay with it? I am an independent man. A lone stallion. I will pave my own way. Without women to bind me down.

Ghanta.

Radha wouldn't let me be even if I tried. I was now stuck with her forever. I felt a noose tighten around my neck. Suddenly I felt claustrophobic. I had done everything she wanted in this relationship. She could at least let me pursue my dream of making money. This argument went on for another half hour, after which I pointed out that I didn't even *have* a job in Dubai and therefore this conversation was silly. She said that it wasn't about the job anymore, but our future and how I treat her. What the fuck! How does my dream of earning more have anything to do with her? She went on to say I don't care about her and how I would leave her if I got a better opportunity and now we had to get married right away.

We had to cut short our argument when my boss called me and said I needed to make a two-hundred slide presentation on our channel for the board of directors by nine o'clock tomorrow morning, and it damn well be good, or he would fire me.

I panicked, and thankfully, when I told Radha what my boss had said, she let the argument rest. Though she did add, 'We still need to talk about this though.' And I absentmindedly nodded because I was wondering whether I could ever really get a job in Dubai since I would never be able to pull off this massive presentation in eleven hours.

I opened up my laptop and asked her to make some tea. It was going to be a long night. I started pulling slides from all the presentations I had ever made, and even some from those that I had copied from others. I managed to put seventy-five slides together like this. Then I went online, copied some other slides, and started filling in data. Several hours passed and Radha dutifully fed me some dinner. She knew I needed some good food, and had ordered from Faasos, comfort food for every man in Mumbai when he is upset, troubled and hungry.

Radha saw me taking a moment to go to the bathroom, and asked what I would do without her if I went to Dubai and had a crisis like this. But I gave her a dirty look and she went to sleep. By eight o'clock the next morning, after many cups of tea, I finally finished the presentation, and felt very proud of myself. I didn't shave but I took a shower and decided to head off to work. I was already late and couldn't afford to rest now.

Radha woke up, saw that I was already ready and asked if I wanted to talk about our problem. I had no idea what she was talking about, and told her so. She went off to the kitchen to make herself a cup of tea and sulk. I picked up my laptop and left.

Now was not the time to pacify the woman in my life. I had to pacify my boss to keep my job. Or I would be heading back to Kolkata with my big tail between my legs and a clingy girlfriend who I would have to introduce to my mother. That was not a happy thought at all.

Little did I know that the next day would be a life-changing one for me. The events of the day would lead me to slowly realize that I needed to find a way out of my current situation, and it would only come about when I wasn't thinking straight.

10

My boss didn't come in till nine-thirty, and this gave me some time to re-check the entire presentation. I thought it looked perfect. If this didn't give me a bonus as big as a house, then nothing I did in this company would ever suffice. And I might as well leave for Dubai. Finally my boss called me into his cabin. He pored over the presentation for fifteen minutes without commenting.

Radha had already sent me ten text messages and five missed calls all of which I'd ignored. Her messages whined about how I'd left without talking to her about her feelings. Women really have no sense of timing. All men want is for women to leave them alone at three important periods in their life: when they're at work, when they're watching TV and when they're in the loo. Is it that hard for them to keep their trap shut at those times?

The boss got to the last slide and looked up at me. I beamed with pride. This was the moment when he was going to congratulate me, and promote me to senior manager. I could already see my new visiting card, the keys to a red Skoda being handed over to me, and my being invited by Arnab to discuss how I changed the game for all marketing people across the country. My boss opened his mouth and said, 'What is this? What the fuck do you call this?'

It didn't sink in for a second. Hadn't he liked it? I had pulled an all-nighter for this. No one else in the organization would have been able to meet that deadline. I stammered and answered, 'Sir...this is the data for the last year of our channel...um...it also has an outlook projected at–'

He interrupted me, saying loudly, 'What shit. What do you know? You don't know anything. Stupid fellow. I have to change everything. It's going to take me ages. Now get out!'

Just then, Radha called *again,* and my phone vibrated for the sixteenth time in my pocket. Therefore, he added, 'And take your moving balls with you.'

I walked out, stunned and dejected. I didn't want to talk to Radha or anyone. I had worked so hard on this deck, hoping that it would be the game changer in my career. It would have helped me prove to my family in Kolkata that I had made it. But my boss had hated it. Why was I even in this organization? Several doubts and self-disparaging thoughts flashed through my brain. I quickly shrugged them off. I was a Bengali. I could not have issues with my confidence. My mother was like Parvati. She had raised me to believe in myself and rule the world. Who was this boss to tell me my deck was no good? I would rebel against him. I would sit and drink tea the whole day and surf porn. Get paid while using company resources for personal work, and while away my time.

Later I was told that my boss hadn't changed anything, but presented the deck just as I had given it to him. The board of directors loved it and praised him for his efforts.

Bastard. He took the credit for making it overnight. He didn't even apologize to me. And my raise was nowhere in sight. My colleagues said that no matter what we did, only time could make you rise in the system. Not merit. I just had to keep going for another ten years like this, before I would be seen or heard and not just shouted at or bossed around.

I went to sulk in the canteen by myself. I ate some breakfast, spoke to Radha, agreeing to everything she said, and was able to cut short the conversation by saying it was all my fault and now I had to go back and salvage this job or we would be on the road tomorrow. She got off the phone then. Women only allow a man to work when they realize that it means that money won't come in if the man hangs around talking to her the whole day.

Some immature colleagues found me and sat around me at the table. 'Hey Obro, aren't your initials OB?'

I shrugged and replied, 'Yeah. Why?'

They burst out laughing as if I'd said something hilarious. 'What? What's so funny?' I asked.

One of them spoke while snorting away, 'It's the name of a tampon, man. Your initials are used for a woman's flow!'

I was mortified. How could my mother do this to me?

I called her up immediately. 'Hello? Bablu? *Kemon acho? Koto din poorey* phone *korchish*.' (How are you? You've called after so long.)

'Ma! I just called you yesterday. And forget all that. How come you named me after a sanitary napkin? How could you do this to me?' I whined, and continued to complain for a few minutes, almost in tears, while she tried to pacify me, saying it was such a noble name and my grandfather had given it to me and he was such a great man and his father was also named Obrobrotin. None of this pleased me in the least. This was no explanation. Just because I came from a generation of OBs didn't make it all right. My great grandfather probably didn't have stupid colleagues in his office calling him a tampon. Bloody shit.

Menon was walking out of the loo when he saw me throw my phone down on the table in anger, after I had hung up on my mother. He nodded to me and I didn't even have the energy to nod back. Bewildered by my behaviour, he came up to me and asked, 'What's up?'

'Nothing,' I answered.

He understood. He said, 'I'm going to head to our drinking adda later. Can you come?'

Yes. This was the exact thing I needed. I wanted to get away from home, office and family. I had needed this for so long. I nodded and he answered, 'Great. It's karaoke night. We should get there early.'

My spirits lifted. Drinking *and* singing? Now this was going to be awesome. I sent Radha a text, telling her I would be working late and not to wait up for me. Although she cribbed and cribbed, I didn't care. Tonight was the night I was going to let my hair down and show the world that I, Obrokranti Banerjee and not OB, was a man who could have fun. He was not bound by a stupid boss and a clingy girlfriend. He was a true-blooded Bengali who was a super-brain and could attract women in hordes.

Tonight was the night. Bring it on!

11

'Whoun more R.D. Burman, please,' I pleaded with the bar owner. It was one o'clock in the morning, and he was trying to shut the bar. I had sung many of the classics in my rich, baritone voice, which everyone wanted to quiet after a few songs. So jealous everyone was. And Menon had sung many English numbers. What an angrez. He didn't know any Hindi numbers and I wanted to show off to the crowd that I was a true Indian. Menon got much more applause than me, but I know people cheer the underdog.

After having many beers and still wanting to sing the night away, I suggested to Menon that we do something wild.

I said brightly, 'Aye Menon. *Ek kaam karta hai*? Muhammad Ali road *mein jaake kabob khata*?' My friends had always made fun of my Hindi, but Menon's Hindi was also quite bad.

He smiled at me and said, 'No man. *Kitna door hai.*' Menon was a man of few words, but the words he chose were powerful. I liked him immensely.

'*Chal na yaar*! Don't be a bore! It's a great drive. I'll sing a few Kishore Kumar numbers now!' I said with a devilish grin. He hadn't heard my rendition of *Choo kar mere mann ko*.

So what if the other people had left when I was singing. He had stayed. I had dazzled him.

Menon looked at me and burst out laughing. 'You're too much *yaar*. *Chal ghar ja*,' he said, dismissing my idea and telling me to go home. Spoilsport. Then I understood. He was very horny and wanted to go home to hump his wife. I got it. I winked at him and said, 'Okay boss. *Biwi* wait *karta hai*.' He shook his head and said, 'Okay *chal*, bye,' while he hailed an auto for me and insisted that my bike would be fine in the office parking lot. But an image of the next morning flashed through my mind. Radha standing on the bed like Ma Kali asking me in which woman's house I had left my bike. Shudder.

'No, no I am fine. I want to ride back home,' I said, going towards my bike. Not that I was afraid of Radha. It was just that I don't like confrontations.

Menon shook his head for a long time. I think he was stuck in the motion. Finally he stopped, stared, pointed his finger at me and then to the stars. I didn't know if he wanted me to guess what he was saying. So I asked, 'Is it a Shah Rukh movie?'

But he clarified, 'Listen to me. Just let the bike be here.' He said we were in no condition to drive and should just head home in an auto. He put me in an auto and gave the driver my address. Then he got into another auto and waved to me. I went back to Radha for the first time in our relationship, reeking of alcohol and in a merry mood. For some reason, I wasn't thinking about how she would react, but instead wondered what my mother would say. I hadn't spoken to her for so long. So I called her. Not thinking about the fact that it was one-thirty in the morning.

The phone rang several times and no one picked up. Then, on the eighteenth ring, my mother picked up the phone and said, 'Hello.' Gee, she sounded just liked me. I must have got my rich baritone voice from her.

'Ma,' I said in a nostalgic mood, 'I miss maach bhaat.'

'Bablu?' my mother asked suspiciously.

I nodded as soberly as possible and replied, 'Who else would it be, Ma? What are you doing?'

My mother burst into a lecture about how bad it was of me not to call her back after I'd hung up in anger. She was most upset. She hadn't eaten anything the whole day and was worried about her health now. She accused me of not worrying about her enough and demanded to know what I had been so busy with the entire day that I couldn't call her back.

So I told her. I told her that I had been up the whole night making a mammoth presentation for an asshole of a boss. And that I was tired of riding a bike and wanted them to send me the family Maruti because I deserved it. I almost told her about Radha being such a possessive bitch, but my super-brain kicked in just at the right time and stopped my verbal diarrhoea. After a long pause she asked in a staccato, 'Bablu! *Tumi koto kheycho?*' (How much have you drunk?)

Now I took a pause. I'd probably had seven or eight large whiskeys. I knew I should play it safe though, so I said, 'Not much. Empty stomach.' My mother bought it. All mothers want to give the benefit of the doubt to their sons. Because their son's behaviour is a direct reflection on them and their mothering skills. If their sons have turned out bad, then they haven't done anything good with their lives. This is the reason why women constantly fight with their daughters-in-law. The woman in a man's life always want to change him. And a mother will always say the finished product that she hands over to the daughter-in-law is perfect since she made him! It's quite embarrassing for a man who thinks he's his own man. He never is.

My mom started giving me a long lecture. How I had become so irresponsible that I didn't care about my own health. She said there was no one looking after me, and like a jackass I had left the family house to pursue a god-forsaken dream in Mumbai where life was so tough. She tried to convince me to come back. She said in Bengali, 'Do you know how well Lengtu is doing here?' These pet names will never leave us I tell you. Even when Shubir becomes the CEO of the biggest business in Kolkata, some jackass of a Bengali from his school will call out, right in the middle of an interview with *Forbes*, and say, '*Aye je* Lengtu. *Kemon acheesh?*' (Hey there, Lengtu! How are you?)

Perhaps it was the Bengali way of keeping intellectuals grounded. Maybe they didn't want anyone to fly too high. Or else, as soon as you've won a Nobel or something, you would think you were great. But if you have people who know you by your pet name, you wouldn't be flaunting the prize around at home, and would do your own laundry. If I have a son, I would give him the pet name Naardu, the white string you use to tie a pyjama that is so essential to keep it up. That will keep him balanced.

Meanwhile, my mother was going on in the background. I realized she'd woken up my father and was saying, '*Gaadha! Jaani na ki korche oikhaney.* (Donkey, don't know what he's up to there.) He's called me drunk!'

I heard him mumble, 'Then just go see what your precious son is up to. You haven't visited him ever.'

My entire buzz went as she agreed with him and said to me, '*Aami kalke aschi.*' I'm coming tomorrow.

What the fuck! She couldn't land up here. Where would I hide Radha?

'*Pagol na ki*? I have so much work, I won't be able to get away from office. And I live with a roommate. There's no place for you. You don't need to come, Ma. I was just missing you. Can't a boy call his mother and tell her she's Parvati to him?'

She softened immediately. 'But why are you drinking so much then?'

'It was only because I was out with friends. And I'm already home. I'll go and sleep now,' I said.

'Okay. If you don't want me to come there, I want you to come see me here. I need to check if you're really okay or you're bluffing.'

Truly, of all the stupid things people have done in the world, I bet no one has ever drunk-dialled their mother. 'I don't have any time. I don't have any leaves,' I said quickly. I was more afraid that Radha would insist on coming with me to Kolkata to meet the parents. And that my mother would have a heart attack when she saw that she was an 'Aw Bangali'. Not like women squeal 'awwww' when they see a cute child. But a NON-Bong. My mother would have the biggest shit fit ever. I would be written out of the family will and that goddamn Lengtu would get all the family inheritance. This wasn't just paranoia talking – it had happened once in my grandfather's generation. His brother had married a south Indian woman. His entire household was aghast. My great grandmother refused to acknowledge her in the house. All the other bahus called her the dark-skinned beauty. And she truly was the loveliest lady in the house. Today all of us speak of how she was the one who managed our family so well. But at that time, my great grandfather disowned his child and gave the entire family property to my grandfather. This was fine by me because ultimately it came to my dad and would be bestowed on me.

Unless I do something major to screw it up. Like marry a NON-Bengali.

Finally, I had to promise to come see her soon. It was the only way she would hang up. And to be honest, I *had* been missing my family. I needed to go see them. And with pujos in a few months, I had been hoping I could head off to Kolkata and do some *masti* with my old school friends without Radha breathing down my neck.

I hung up, paid the auto driver a hundred bucks. Argued with him. Paid him the remaining hundred bucks. Went upstairs. Unlocked my door. Went to the bathroom. Ignored Radha who was sitting up in bed with folded arms. Curled up in bed and went to sleep. I knew I'd sort things out in the morning. I would explain how I was forced to go out drinking, and that my phone battery died. It would all be okay. By the time I fell asleep, I had even forgotten that I'd called my mother. It seemed like a dream anyway.

12

I woke up very late the next day and called in sick at work. I couldn't go in reeking of alcohol. Plus, I had a massive hangover. I drank some water and went back to sleep. I vaguely heard Radha saying something, but in my state I might actually have said, 'Shut up and leave me alone.' I swear to God I shall never ever treat a woman so badly again. It must have been the alcohol.

Radha went off to sulk. I woke up at around two o' clock, feeling better. Until I realized that Radha had made just enough lunch for herself, and hadn't left anything for me. When I asked her about it, she said she wanted to know where I had been and why I hadn't taken any of her calls the previous evening. Only then did I remember that I had chosen to ignore Radha's fifty-seven calls, though I felt I had been very clever by sending her an SMS saying I was busy at work and unable to take her call. But because I had walked into the apartment completely drunk and humming a song, she guessed that I'd lied to her.

I really have no clue why women want to kill any buzz a man has. I mean a hangover is hard enough to handle. We're puking. We are hoping that our sanity comes back and the damn throbbing headache will go away. But we're recollecting the wonderful night we had. One of the best that we can remember. For a long time. In the midst of all this, they want to talk about our behaviour. Are they completely mad?

'If you don't tell me what happened last night you see what I'll do to you,' threatened Radha with her arms folded. For a fleeting moment, I wondered if she was going to leave. The happiness lasted only for a second, as I quickly realized what she was talking about: that she would deny me sex. And that was worse. Having a woman invade your life and then to not get any sex is the worst thing that could happen to a man. Men tolerate women because at the end of all that nagging is some nakedness. Imagine if you have to hear her complain and shout the whole day long and on top of that she refuses to remove her clothes and give you any sex. That's marriage. And I wasn't married yet!

'Okay, okay,' I said trying to formulate words while the *thump thump* in my head grew stronger. 'I was with Menon at a bar.' Radha's eyes popped out and she shrieked, 'AT A BAR? DRINKING?'

I nodded meekly.

Then she went on to scream in a very loud voice about how I didn't care about her at all. This was totally unnecessary. A man needs to go out. We need to have fun. We can't be chained to a house and a woman all the time. I thought I should voice this aloud until the first sensible thought in twenty-four hours came to my head – don't. But the alcohol had permeated too deeply into my thick skull and had loosened my brain waves and tongue.

Hence, I said the next thing that automatically came into

my head, 'You know if you let me just have a boys' night out once in a while, or call my friends over, I would never have to lie to you.'

Her eyes almost fell out of her socket as she said, 'SO THIS IS MY FAULT?'

'Oh God. I wish you would stop screaming. I have a horrible headache and you're not helping with all that shouting.'

People talk about their life flashing before their eyes, moments before their death. I had thought it was a myth. Until I experienced it for myself. Radha's face contorted into a horrible shape. Like Ma Durga before she slew Mahishashur. It was not pretty.

I needed to be the boss of my life. Take some affirmative action. I had no clue how. Maybe I should ask my father. He had always taken affirmative action by telling everyone around what he wanted. And it was just magically done. I got the feeling that my mother always planted the idea of what he wanted though.

'Please go make me some food. I'm starving,' I blurted out, deciding this was the moment to start taking charge of things.

Radha looked at me for a second and then quietly walked towards the kitchen. For a moment, I thought I had shown her. Then she returned with all the vegetables from the fridge. And dumped them on me. 'What would you like to eat? Some bhindi? Gobhi? Tinde?'

Actually, I thought, I would like to have some maach bhaat. But with cold, raw vegetables on my head, I didn't think it was the correct time to say that. So I silently cursed her and ordered a Domino's pizza for myself. Women are supposed to be good at cooking. I mean, I'm all for them being financially independent. In fact, I would love it if I could sit at home while they went out and worked. I would support my wife wholeheartedly in being the breadwinner. But if you're going to sit at home, at least make some food, woman! That's your role. My role is to bring in money to manage the house and occasionally pay taxes and fix the AC when it breaks down. It's all clear cut.

Radha didn't see it that way. She said she made the decision to stay at home because, with her delicate looks, she could get harassed at a workplace. Delicate, my ass. No employer wanted to hire her because she would dominate him and crush his ego like an elephant on egg shells. Apparently she had been working in a call centre before she met me. She had the night shift, and she didn't like it. She went to her boss and asked that she be transferred to the day shift. The boss refused. She slapped a sexual harassment case against him. She was fired, without a recommendation letter. And since then it had been difficult for her to find a job she liked or a boss she could manage, and she decided to take a sabbatical and just sit at home. She said she didn't need a job. She had me. The bakra. I provided everything for her to sit at home and watch TV.

The doorbell rang. Food. Men have had a longer relationship with Domino's than they have with any woman in their lives. It was exactly what they needed, when they needed it and delivered wherever they wanted it. Why couldn't women be like that?

After I finished eating, I lay on the couch and switched on the TV. Radha couldn't bear it anymore. So she said, 'Can't you see I'm giving you the silent treatment? I haven't spoken to you for so long!'

Honestly I think 'the silent treatment' is the best thing that could happen to a man. I prayed that Radha would give it to me more often.

I sighed and said, 'I'm sorry. I didn't notice.'

'You're just not bothered anymore. I demand an explanation. An apology.'

An apology for what? That I went out? I wasn't sorry about that. That I got drunk? I had enjoyed it. That I lied to her? Okay maybe I shouldn't have done that.

'I'm sorry baby. It's been a rough week. And I really wanted to relax. Please forgive me,' I said with partial truth. It *had* been a tough week with my boss screaming at me after my all-nighter. And this was the time I expected her to understand.

'I didn't think that you needed the boys to relax. I thought I was enough for you. But apparently I'm not!' she said sarcastically, and put on her shoes to go for a walk. I called after her with a weak, 'Radha, please.' But I knew she wouldn't go far. She didn't have any money. She just wanted to me to run after her and coax her back into my arms. Women read too many Mills & Boon novels and have such silly expectations from men. That's why we all hate Shah Rukh Khan and Mills & Boon heroes.

But since I knew what women wanted, I would have gone after Radha had it not been for my throbbing head and my stomach so full with a large chicken pizza. I was immobilized. Which was a good thing because it meant I had the whole house to myself. For a change.

I decided to do the one thing that every man dreams of doing at home but can't, because they're always surrounded by spouses or maids. Get naked. Well I didn't really want to masturbate. But I did want to check out my balls. I had read somewhere that after a binge night of drinking, your balls shrink. So I walked into the bathroom and checked.

They *had* shrunk. Or maybe it was just my mind playing tricks on me. I noticed some spots but I couldn't see them clearly because of all the fuzz. So I decided to trim my hair. I walked into the kitchen, naked, to get a pair of scissors. See, this was the life. I could do what I wanted in my house. Unfortunately, the woman from across the apartment was in the kitchen at the same time and saw me. I gave her a grin. Her jaw fell to the floor and she quickly ran out of her kitchen. Heh heh. Stupid builders in Mumbai would finally realize that you need to have houses that face *away* from your neighbours, not *into* their flats. Bloody *Rear Window* syndrome they suffer from. (It's a reference to Alfred Hitchcock. What a funny last name he had. Great director though.)

I went back to the bathroom, stood over the pot and began the task super carefully. Women might say it's quite a chore to wax every month, but let me tell you, trimming your balls requires precision and attention. One wrong move and you could...aaahhh...don't even think about it. I thought I was a doing a great job. Radha would love me all clean down under. I could just imagine her moaning and groaning with my smooth scrotum. Otherwise the woman plays with it like loose change in her hands for a few seconds and lies down. Expects me to do all the work. Bleddy. Today I would show her the new me and she would be impressed. In fact, for future use, I could even buy an electronic trimmer. Hmmm...that seemed like a good idea.

Slam!

Shit. Radha was back. And the bathroom door was open.

And I was naked, with hair lying all around the pot, and a pair of scissors in my hands. I don't know what happened to me, but in my hurry to shut the bathroom door before she could find me, by accident I poked my balls with the scissors.

'FUUUUUUCCCCCCKKKKKKK!' I screamed, dropped the scissors and held my dignity with both my hands as I lay on the bathroom floor crying like a baby.

Radha rushed in and saw my state. 'What the hell were you doing?'

In between sobs I replied, 'I was trying to do something nice for you.'

'Shaving your balls is doing something nice for me?' she asked sarcastically. Women have no appreciation I tell you.

'I wasn't *shaving*,' I said. I should try shaving next time though, I thought. It might actually be safer. But fuck it. If she wasn't going to be happy with all my effort, why should I risk injury to my family jewels? Let the jungle be.

She ran to the fridge and got me some ice wrapped in my handkerchief and I placed it there tenderly. Then after a few minutes, I was able to get up and walk to the sofa. And there I sat in my naked splendour, with ice on my balls. I realized that the cut was not as bad as it could have been. Thank God, I didn't have to go to the hospital. That would have been embarrassing.

The cook rang the doorbell in the evening and I finally went in for a shower. Thankfully Radha hadn't nagged me the whole day about taking a bath. She can go on and on about showering. Men are not supposed to be clean, I told her. They're hunters, gatherers, farmers. They're not obsessed about hygiene. That's a woman's domain. Honestly, I really wish that male-female domains were outlined clearly from the beginning. It would make it much easier for women to understand who had to do what.

The cook had made some food by the time I came out of my shower. I had some puri bhaaji and decided to sleep again.

It had been a most tiring day. Radha was still annoyed with me, but seeing me in pain and how annoyed I was with lack of food, she decided to refrain from saying too much.

I knew tomorrow I had to do something with my life. I had to take a stand. I was going to figure out where my life was going. But for now, all I wanted was some sleep.

13

There are two types of women in this world. One who will tell you exactly when their birthday is, what they want and how much it will cost, thus saving you sleepless nights wondering what you should buy her. The other will not only not remind you when her birthday is, but when you ask what she wants, will say 'Surprise me!' Then, my friend, you are truly and most completely screwed.

Any man will tell you that the girlfriend/wife's birthday is the most dangerous day in a relationship. Because, more often than not, you will forget it. And even if you do remember it, you always buy the wrong present, not wish her on time, and it will be a weekday, which means your boss is burning your ass at the other end while she is waiting for you to get home and take her out for a romantic meal.

Radha loves surprises for her birthday. And I hate giving them. Last year, I had made it infinitely clear (because it was the beginning of our relationship and I could get away with such things) that either I could give her money to buy a present or I could take her out for dinner. But on my salary I could not afford both. So she had opted to have a nice romantic meal. I took her to a lovely restaurant in Andheri

West and bought her balloons on the way back. She had been quite happy then. Well, almost happy. Two months later she had started complaining that I hadn't bought her a present and the place we'd gone to was cheap and how could I have bought her balloons, she wasn't ten years old, and at least I should have got flowers! Jesus! Women! You can never please them. Whatever you do, they're never happy.

So this year I asked her the same question in the quarter of her birthday. Which meant around August, so she could give me a hint if her birthday was in the next month or not. She said, 'There's still some time, but I'm glad you're already thinking about it.' Now at this point I could not ask, 'When is it?' I would be hit over the head with the rolling pin used to make chapattis in the house.

So I put a reminder on my mobile and asked her every other week, and around September she finally said, 'I know, it's on Thursday and I haven't planned anything. You surprise me!'

Thursday? Thursday? My mind began to panic. Did I have enough money saved? What could I buy her? A restaurant outing would cost at least one or two grand. And a present on top of that? I wondered if I could get away with staying back in office till late on the pretext of work, and just getting her flowers.

On Monday morning, on my way to work, I stopped at a florist.

'Twenty rupees for one rose stem. And you need to buy a dozen for a bouquet to look nice. And fifty rupees for all the *hara pata* that I add to decorate it,' replied the florist when I asked about the cheapest bouquet that would look nice.

'Or you can give these lovely pink lilies. You can match it

with this bird of paradise. The whole bouquet I can give you for seven hundred and fifty,' he said putting the bunch together to show how gorgeous it would look. Like I cared. I was having a mini heart attack right there in the shop. Fuck! Seven hundred and fifty rupees? I could buy two quarters and some chakna at the place in Andheri East where Menon and I had gone. And the flowers would die in a couple of days in any case! But Menon and memories would remain forever.

I walked away from the florist and decided I would buy her a nice present. Ninety per cent of women love jewellery. But if you're broke like me, then you need to figure out what else they like. Now here, my friends, is the problem. If you have been paying attention to your girlfriend...let me stop and laugh – who pays attention? Anyway, if you have been a diligent boyfriend and been paying attention to your girlfriend's likes and dislikes, and noticed what she has and doesn't have, desires and really needs, you would know that there are a wide variety of things you can buy her which she would love as a present.

Some women are into camping, trekking, and you can buy them a cheap watch that lights up in the dark. They'll probably be happy with that. Never buy a woman a household item. Even though they buy loads of sheets, cushion covers and stock pillows like there's a shortage likely, if you buy it for them as a birthday present, they'll be offended and say something like, 'Do you want to domesticate me? Do you think I should just sit at home and change cushion covers?'

Once my father made the grave error of saying, 'But isn't that what you do every day in any case?'

My mother didn't cook for him for a week. We had to order in food. Till my father apologized and bought her jewellery. The next year he bought her a food processor. She walked out. That man never learns. And since then, she just takes the money from my father and buys whatever she wants. She's the first woman in the family who has understood that the man has no clue and that she needs to always be in charge when it comes to presents. It comes with age, I suppose. The more you stay with each other, the more you realize that your expectations need to be lowered if you want to live peacefully.

It had just been two years for Radha and me. The peace wasn't coming anytime soon. I finally decided to take her to a fancy place for dinner. But on the eve of her birthday, she said, 'I want a present this year. Whatever you think I deserve. Surprise me!'

I was royally screwed. I asked Menon in office, 'Dude, what do you think is a good present for my girlfriend? Her birthday is tomorrow.'

Menon turned around from his computer on which he was playing solitaire, and said, 'Are you serious? You waited this long to buy her a gift?'

'It's tomorrow!' I reminded the moron. I had a full twenty-four hours to shop.

'Why didn't you buy something when the sales were on?' he asked.

'What are you? A woman? No righteous man goes to a sale! So many women jostling around to buy the same thing and save a few hundred bucks. Please. I'm never going for a sale.'

'So many women pushing and shoving, you in the centre, getting squashed. It's a Thai sandwich massage, man. You don't have to do anything!' Menon said, his eyes twinkling.

I could see his point suddenly, and we wasted a full ten minutes discussing whether we should go to Thailand and get sandwich massages done. I finally returned to the topic and asked him again, 'So, do you have any suggestions for a gift?'

'What's your budget?' Menon asked, while typing on his keyboard: 'what to buy women as birthday gifts'.

I thought about it, and with the salary I had, the money I sent back home and the expenses mounting, I could only come up with one number, 'Five hundred.'

Menon turned around again and looked at me, 'Dude. For that much you won't get shit.'

I glared at him. Obviously he was making far more than I was or wasn't spending as much. 'Well what should it be?' I asked, wanting to know what the current rate of a present was.

'Perfumes are at least three or four grand. Jewellery is much more. Clothes cost at least a grand for a suit or dress. Shoes can cost anything from a grand to ten grand.'

'Can I buy her a book?' I said, thinking I was a genius for coming up with such a great idea.

'You might as well buy her onions. You'll get about five kilos. And then you'll get about a lifetime worth of tears,' Menon said getting up and heading for the loo. I followed him. I didn't want to lose the thread of the conversation. 'You have about an hour to shop,' he continued. 'After work you have to go to the mall and find something that she will like and that will fit in your budget. You know how tough that is? I went out with a woman for five years and every year I tried to find something nice. The time taken to get the perfect present is directly proportional to figuring out you're completely fucked with whatever you buy in any case.'

I don't know why Menon took off his pants while peeing. It was always unnerving for me to see his butt cheeks. It was difficult for me to maintain eye contact with his hairy ass on display. No wonder the woman left him after five years. She wasn't sick of his useless gifts, she was tired of touching his hairy bum.

But I needed help. With the grim picture he had drawn, I wanted him to come along and give me suggestions – even if they were useless – rather than walk around aimlessly in the women's department of Lifestyle as if I were a man stranded in a desert looking for an oasis. 'Please Menon,' I begged, 'Please come with me. I'll buy you a drink later.'

At the mention of the free drink, Menon agreed to come and help me choose a gift. But, he said, he wouldn't help for more than five minutes because otherwise the single ladies at the store would think he was shopping for his own girlfriend and he didn't want to give them the impression that he was taken. The idiot. As if anyone in Lifestyle would look at him and drop everything to spend their entire life with the hairy ass.

So off we went to a mall post work to buy Radha a present. Little did we know the night would end in complete disaster.

As always, one more guide. This one prepared while nursing a hangover that split my head open, much like Moses parted the sea.

Five Things to Buy Your Girlfriend if You're Broke

1. Books. Books can be nice and cheap, and every woman likes having books around to show people how well-read

she is. You can get the entire range of Chetan Bhagat books for less than five hundred bucks. And most women love him.

2. Bath products. Nice smelling foamy gels and lotions are always a hit. You don't need to go in for high-end products; local brands are good too. Ask the shop people to package it nicely with ribbons and bows. Women love pretty packaging. And it makes them feel special to open things up.

3. Bags. Women love bags. They can't get enough of them. And they change their bags every week. Hence the more they have, the merrier they are. Find a cheap place in your local market and get a good-looking bag from there. Gym bags, clutches, slings, whatever shit they're called. Wrap it up nicely. Add a bow.

4. Photo frames. Women love selfies, and they love having their photographs in nice-looking frames. They can place photos of themselves all around the house where everyone can see them. It shows who the master of the house is.

5. Wine. A nice, cheap bottle of wine is better than no wine. First of all, it's booze – it will be drunk. Secondly, when you gift wine it shows that you think she's high class. In her head, she's better than a woman who drinks beer. Thirdly, she might be horny after the alcohol and you get to score! Win-win!

14

Five minutes turned into five hours. I've never had so much fun shopping. Menon took me to a mall that had all the biggest brands. Of course we didn't go into any shop that didn't have a sale going on. When we were booted out of three stores for asking what I could buy my girlfriend for five hundred rupees, we became quite dejected. When had all the prices gone up so much? How could I afford anything on seventeen thousand rupees a month?

I decided to increase my budget to a thousand rupees. But first, we needed to eat. We headed to the food court and decided to have the cheapest thing there, McDonald's burgers. It turned into an expensive affair though, because Menon was so distracted by a girl that he walked straight into an old man and dropped his Happy Meal. I had to buy him another one because he claimed it was my fault – I had brought him to the mall in the first place.

'She was completely hot though,' he said smiling. 'I think she went to get an ice cream. Give me some money, yaar. I want to get her phone number.'

I shook my head and said, 'Your girl. Your money. I need to still buy Radha a present.'

Menon went up to the girl and came back with his hand on his cheek. 'What happened?' I asked, already knowing the answer as the gesture looked very familiar.

'The pick-up line,' is all he said, as it is the one thing that every man understands. If the first thing you say to a woman does not come out all right, you would make the worst impression on her and then have to start all over with someone else. It is the five seconds we have to make an impression. And in those five seconds, our fate is sealed. Would she sleep with you or slap you.

I burst out laughing. I am now the expert on pick-up lines. 'You should have come to me first,' I said. 'Have you tried – "Hey baby, you must be a light switch because every time I see you, I'm turned on"?'

Menon looked at me with a blank expression. Okay so that hadn't worked on him. I tried another one and a few more.

'I wanna live in your socks because I want to be with you every step of the way.'

'Is there an airport nearby or is that my heart taking off?'

'My love for you is like diarrhoea. I just can't hold it in.'

Menon and I had started walking to the escalators by then and he turned around then and said, 'Dude, if you've got a woman with any of that shit, I say stick with her, man. Coz you ain't getting another one anytime soon.'

I stuck my tongue out at him, 'As if your pick-up line worked, Mr Travolta!'

He smiled and said, 'It did. It was her boyfriend who saw her talking to me who slapped me. But I'm pretty sure she's into me!'

I was shocked. How could this happen? 'What did you say?' I asked incredulously.

'I said I spilt my entire meal because I couldn't keep my eyes off her and even though I didn't have any money to buy her an ice cream, I just wanted to spend ten seconds in a line standing behind her so I could feel complete that I had seen such a beauty in my life.'

I laughed my ass off at that. 'And she bought it? Dude, you two are made for each other then. Mr Bullshit and Ms Gullible belong together.'

He smiled and said, 'Right?!'

But before we could go back to the topic of women and what to buy for Radha, we got distracted by the most wondrous sight in the mall. Something that all men need, to channel the inner child in them. Something that they never give up on, no matter what happens in their lives. Something that lives on through puberty, *Playboy* or pathetic lives. Video games!

'The new *Grand Theft Auto V*,' Menon said reverently. Men will not remember which book they read last, any childhood memory that shaped them into who they are, the MBA stuff that they mugged up for hours for an exam, or their children's birthdays, or how they met their wives. But they will always know when their favourite video game came out and their last score while playing the old version.

'I need to beat my score,' Menon said, looking at it with more desire than he would while going through a *Playboy*.

I looked at it more fondly than I've ever looked at Radha. We stared at it for a few more minutes till a woman came up to us and asked, 'Would you like to play it?'

Menon looked at me. I looked at Menon. To buy this would mean we would need to sell a kidney. But to play this once, just once, would mean our life's ambition was fulfilled.

Not a single thought of Radha's present entered my head. 'Yes!' I said with a whoop of delight. So the woman helped us get on the mat, loaded the game, made us wear 3-D glasses, put something in our hands so we could manoeuvre the game and we got on for the ride of our lives.

It was the best twenty minutes of my life. Like women compare the best orgasm to chocolate, men compare their best orgasm to a video game. Except we never say it out loud, otherwise we would never get sex again.

After the video game, we were on a high.

'We need a drink, man!' Menon said, and I agreed.

We headed on my bike to the nearest quarter joint (where you can order a quarter pint of alcohol, and not just singles/doubles), and laughed the entire way there – at our pick-up lines, at the woman who didn't look like Lara Croft at all, basically, at everything, because we were happy.

After a few hours of drinking and eating, it finally dawned on me. It was almost midnight and I hadn't got Radha a present. Nor was I close enough home to make it back in time to wish her.

'Fuck!' I said with rising fear. 'I have to leave.' And with great trepidation I looked at my phone as it went from 11:59 to 00:00. The countdown to my doom had begun.

And all I could do was send a message to Radha saying: 'Happy birthday sweetheart.'

15

There are points in a man's life when he knows he's screwed up. Usually, he has no clue what he's done wrong. But there are rare moments when he does actually know. And in those moments, he never claims he was right. All he says is, 'Sorry.' Basically, he says it to get laid again. Guilt, regret and apologies could get you back in the relationship, and more importantly, in the sack. Or, my friend, you'll see yourself out in the cold.

Radha locked me out of the house. My house. Where I paid rent. Not she. And I sat outside knocking on the door gently – because I didn't want the neighbours to complain – begging for her to let me in. 'Please baby, I had gone to get your present and forgot all about the time. Please let me come inside and explain.' At first, there was total silence and I didn't know if she was so distraught that I hadn't wished her that maybe she'd committed suicide.

Then I heard her shuffle around, probably looking for a sledgehammer to knock me down with, and then finally, from the other side of the door she said, 'The stores shut at nine o'clock. It's midnight.'

'I got lost.'

Really. Men come up with the stupidest excuses when there's a crisis in their relationship. And we desperately cling to hope that the woman will buy the stupid reason. Just so that we can get laid again.

Radha opened the door just a crack and glared at me. I was all ready to walk inside and make up with her. She had forgiven me. Hallelujah! But she held out her hand and said, 'Okay, give it to me.'

'I...' Fumbling, I dug into my pockets, hoping something would emerge, like in *The Lord of the Rings*. But all I could find were chits of papers from parking at malls, train tickets, bills from bars and a phone number I didn't recognize. Crap.

'Well?' she asked.

'Radha, you know how much I love you,' I said, hoping to gain some sympathy from the stony-faced devil. But she was unrelenting. I racked my brains for a good excuse. 'It was just that Menon was unwell na...'

She looked straight through me, 'So you went drinking?'

I shook my head left and right a few times more than necessary and she knew I was lying. If our minds don't fail us, our bodies definitely will.

'So you forgot my birthday? Didn't get me a present and went drinking with that ass Menon?'

I nodded my head without thinking. That's when she slammed the door shut on me again.

Then I shook my head and said, 'No, I did remember your birthday.' But it was too late. I slunk to the floor. Radha opened it a crack again and asked, 'So you remembered my birthday but went drinking with Menon anyway?'

I finally shut up. I forced my body to remain still, neither nodding nor shaking my head. When women are screaming at you, it's best to not move. Pretend that you're invisible and hope that the problem will go away on its own.

'I don't know what's worse! That you didn't remember and went off or that you did and you went anyway.'

I really didn't see the difference but apparently it was causing Radha's face to become all red with rage. What's the big deal? So I wasn't there at midnight. It wasn't as if her birthday had *finished*. It was just beginning. I had a full twenty-four hours to make it up. What was she getting so furious about?

'What do you have to say for yourself?'

Oh drat. This is one of the worst things a woman can ask a man. We really don't know what to say for ourselves. We are clueless. If we knew better, we wouldn't have done what we did. If we'd learnt something from this, we wouldn't do it again. But the chances are that this mistake will get repeated like the several other ones we make because, honestly, at this point, all we want is for our girlfriend to stop being angry with us so we can just get back to our normal existence.

'Please Radha. Just let me in. I'll make it up to you tomorrow. I'll take the day off and we can go shopping.' That's the magic word. Shopping. If a man is ever in doubt about how to please a woman – take her shopping. It will leave a gaping hole in your wallet but at least you will not be alone with your hand for the rest of your life.

Radha opened the door and smiled for the first time since Monday. 'Really? You mean that?' she asked. And my body relented. I nodded. She threw her arms around me and said, 'Then you're forgiven. For now.' Thank God!

But that wasn't the end of it. When I was crawling into bed, ready to pass out from the exhaustion of the fight, the long day and the madness of the mall with Menon, Radha turned to me and said, 'I want to talk about why you did what you did. Just because you're taking me shopping doesn't mean it's all okay.'

Aarrghh!

I turned away and said what all men have been taught to say when they're stuck in sticky situations, 'I promise to never do it again. I'm truly sorry. Let's talk about it in the morning while I'm buying you something nice.'

Within moments I was snoring, and it was too late for Radha to realize that I hadn't even wished her happy birthday. Something I would hear about for the rest of the year.

The next morning, Radha seemed incredibly happy.

'Oh baby you didn't tell me you were going to have the present delivered!'

I was stunned. What was she talking about?

But there in my drawing room sat a massive, white teddy bear as big as a six-year-old child – and that rightfully should have been owned only by a six-year-old. But Radha picked it up and cuddled it happily.

'Have you met my shweetu weetu Mr Teddy Links?'

Now here's a thing about women. Most of them grow out of the stuffed toy stage at about seven. But there are many who will continue with this fetish well into adulthood, and the easiest thing to get this kind of woman is a stuffed toy. When she is angry with you, a stuffed toy will always dissipate the temper. And as soon as she gets a stuffed toy, she'll give it a name and treat it like a little baby. That's why if a woman has stuffed toys in her house, you may want to run. This woman wants to have children, and lots of them. Real quick.

'I'm so glad you're happy. This was my surprise,' I said lying through my teeth. I saw my phone blinking and went to pick it up. Menon had messaged. 'I ordered something from Archies from your side. They said they would deliver it in the morning. You owe me.'

I felt my heart fall madly in love with Menon. He had saved me.

Throughout the day, Radha made me talk to that goddamn toy as if it were our child. She insisted we take it with us when we went out for lunch as well. But thankfully I didn't have to take her shopping or buy any more presents.

(Great insight: When in doubt, buy any random present for a birthday – women will generally go and exchange it later anyway. But landing up empty-handed will never get you laid.)

16

Porn is a man's birthright. And he shall have a stash of it in every lifetime. I keep mine on my laptop, password protected. A few years ago I used to have my porn in CDs and magazines that were kept in an old duffel bag on top of my cupboard at home. But one day Ma decided to clean my old room.

She called Shibu da, our trusted servant since 1887 (ya, he was that old), and asked him to bring down the duffel bag so the tops of the cupboards could be dusted. The old man climbed up a rickety ladder, and zipped open the bag first, hoping there would be some alcohol that he could steal. But he saw the CDs and magazines and told my mother, 'There's nothing in this. Give me a cloth, I'll clean around it and just keep it here.' Later he blackmailed me and I had to give him half my collection along with a bottle of Bagpiper's whiskey. But at least he saved me the humiliation of dealing with my mother.

Mothers are always in denial about their sons' sexual interests. When Lengtu wet his bed, his mother said, 'He must have been drinking water and it spilt at night in the dark.' Horny bastard had started early, dreaming of the girls in his class who had started developing breasts.

When boys begin to masturbate, all mothers believe that they're just trying to shave in the bathroom. 'That's why he's taking so long,' they rationalize to themselves, 'because he needs to shave his moustache.'

And when boys come home at night after bonking the girls at 'socials' in school, the mothers will say, 'How can my son ever do something so horrendous? He worships Ma Durga. He would never do something so vile.'

So if a mother actually catches her son with porn, it would be the worst thing for their relationship. She would have to stop being in denial and he would never look up from her feet.

When I was in college my large collection of porn was passed around. Everyone wanted the name of my CD dealer but I refused to give it. Finally, after a few bribes were given, I revealed the number and all of us began to exchange CDs. It was more economical because, after some time, the CDs got so bad that we had to throw them.

Nowadays all my friends have external hard drives to store their porn. We never delete porn. It's sacrilege. We only build on it. If we stacked all the porn movies we have side by side, we would encircle the world more times than Superman did in the movie.

It was just when I had saved enough money to buy an external hard drive that calamity struck. I had left my laptop at home and gone out for a walk. Now this was a bad idea to begin with. Bengalis aren't meant to exercise. Bong boys are naturally fit or plump. Take it or leave it. You marry us for our intellectual prowess and our stamina in bed. You don't find many Bengali men with six pack abs. Because we're using up the six pack of beer while we're watching the match on weekends.

So when Radha commented that I'd put on weight, I scoffed and asked her to pass me another beer. The next thing I knew, I was out the door with sneakers that had mould on them, my apartment door shutting on my face. I wasn't allowed inside for a full hour with the instruction that I had 'better be sweaty from the walk'. Crap. There went my plan to order beer and watch the match at Banjara.

So I walked all around my complex, waving at a few children who started crying and ran to their mummies, not realizing that I'd left my laptop open and on in my room at home. With Radha.

Now here's the thing. In my defence, I had used a really complicated password. And labelled one of the porn folders 'Personal Don't Touch'. So, ideally, no one should touch it, and more importantly, try to hack into it. There are some spaces that are extremely private to a man. An old bag on top of a cupboard, and a folder that's labelled 'personal' should fit into the category.

I rang the bell, and waited for a few minutes. Nothing. So I rang again and again till Radha finally came to the door. An expression that was a strange mixture of anger and disappointment was on her face. I was unable to comprehend it. Did she want sex to cheer her up? But by now I knew enough to play safe rather than be sorry. 'What's up with you? I walked a full hour. Just because you told me to!'

Radha slapped my face and burst into tears. 'Ow!' I exclaimed, holding my face. 'Fine, I'll never go for a walk again. What's wrong with you?' She pointed to the laptop on the dining table, a porn video on pause.

Okay now I didn't know what to say. I went up to the dining table and switched it off. Then I turned around and spoke. 'How did you get into the file?'

'Is that the point?' Radha screamed.

Wasn't *I* supposed to be mad? She had broken into my personal file and was going through my personal things. *I* was supposed to be injured party here. It was my fuckin' right to scream at her. And she was taking even that away from me!

'You have a stupid password. Anyone can guess it. How could you? How could you cheat on me?' Radha said, lunging forward to hit me again.

I ducked and ran to the end of the small room. 'What are you talking about? It's just porn! Every man has some.'

'Am I not good enough for you? Do you need to watch this filth?'

I shook my head and she misunderstood and screamed, 'What? I'm not good enough for you? How dare you! I would have you know that you are lucky to have me. I am a catch.'

I wondered for a second if I could throw back the catch, but then a thought flooded over me – maybe I would be left with only porn in my life and that would be really sad.

'Baby,' I pleaded, 'I'm sorry I collect porn. It was there before you came along.'

'Don't lie. This one says you downloaded it yesterday.'

That was true. It was a new Nicole something video and she was too hot for me not to download. I was planning on exchanging it with Menon for some celebrity porn he had got recently.

'I want you to delete all of it.'

Radha had said the worst thing a man could ever hear. Even worse than that he had a few weeks to live. If there was no porn in a man's life, there was nothing. Porn helped us deal with bad bosses, long hours of work, nagging partners, over-priced restaurants, and India losing to Pakistan in a cricket match. Porn gave us relief in more ways than one. How could she ask me to delete it? This was a collection I had built over years. Long hours of trawling the net to find the perfect clips. Browsing through millions of sites to find the ideal ones. This was a body of work that I was actually proud of. I could show off my porn collection to my friends if the time arose. And she was asking me to delete it?

Hell no!

'Radha,' I said calmly, 'I'm not going to delete it. It's sacrilege. We just don't do that.'

'We?' she asked with her hands on her hips. 'Who's we? I don't care about we. I care about you. And I think this is dirty filthy shit. It's degrading to women. And it's downright insulting to me.'

'How?' I asked.

'How?' she retorted.

Really, if she was going to ask me everything back then there was no point of this conversation. 'Ya, how?' I repeated.

'Because you think I will do all this stuff with you. And when I can't, then you blame me for not being the perfect girlfriend.'

'You can't even do the simple things like take off your clothes when I ask you to. Why would I even suggest a blow job in an elevator?' My line of questioning wasn't going to make me win any argument, but it could at least put some thoughts in her head.

'I don't care. I want you to delete it.'

I sat down on the sofa, feeling like I needed to stand my ground. I might regret it later, but I had to exert my authority for the first time in my life. Porn was important to me. It

wasn't affecting my daily life. I wasn't a porn addict who
spent all day watching videos – even though the thought of
that did sound amazing. I was a responsible adult who
worked and looked after my girlfriend. I was not going to let
go of my values so easily. Porn is every man's freedom to jerk
off. I could not have that taken away from me.

'What if I don't?' I asked.

Radha could not believe I'd said that. 'WHAT?' she roared.
'What do you mean you won't?'

I rephrased my words in a kinder fashion, 'I meant to say,
baby, I will promise not to watch it. I will be faithful only to
you and never ask you to do the things that porn stars do.
But please don't ask me to delete it. Just pretend it's not
there. It was a present given by some friends and there's
nothing I can do about it.'

Radha's stance softened ever so slightly as she replied,
'Some presents can be thrown away, you know.'

I came up to her and gave her a tight hug, 'I know, but
this one can't. Let's just suppose it's there and I will never see
it again. I have done everything you say till now. See I even
went for a walk to get into shape for you. Please let this be.'

I tried all my usual tricks – suggesting I take her shopping
and buy her a present, but it wouldn't work. Finally, I said,
'How about I cook for you to make it up?'

Radha was as surprised as I was that it came out of my
mouth. 'You'll do that?'

'Of course. It's easy. What would you like to have for
dinner?'

Radha thought about it and came up with something so
complicated even a chef in the Maurya Sheraton wouldn't
have known how to go about it. 'Escargot.'

'No, we're not getting on a flight. Think of something that's easier, Radha!'

She shrugged and said, 'Anything non-vegetarian.'

I went to the kitchen and said, 'Well let's see what we have here then.'

And like Nigella, I started taking things out of the fridge, smelling them and putting them on the counter. Radha followed me and smiled. 'Do you need any help, Master Chef?'

'Are there any onions and tomatoes chopped?'

She showed me that there were some in the fridge where the maid had kept them.

'Then I don't need your help. You go and relax and I'll make you a fabulous meal.' She gave me a big kiss and went to switch on the TV.

I immediately called my mother to ask her how to make chicken. Most men's go-to recipes are their mother's. They will call them up or their cook from their native places and ask what goes in a dish. No one really looks up the internet or flips on a channel to see how to cook a dish. And many men don't remember recipes even after they've made it several times.

My mom was impressed that I was trying to eat healthy and cooking for myself. I didn't tell her it was present to pacify my girlfriend who had found my porn collection. I scribbled down whatever she said and got to work. I took me a long time to cook, partly because I was constantly checking my phone for mails and chatting on Whatsapp with the office boys group I was on. They had recently included me after Menon put in a good word. I didn't want to disappoint them by not replying just because I was busy cooking.

In the process I burnt the rice.

Radha entered the kitchen and saw the white rice turning brown.

'Look at this mess, Obro! This kitchen will take me two days to clean!'

I looked around. Obviously there would be a mess. A man was cooking. He needed a work station, and he didn't clean up after himself. That was for the sous chef. The head chef just made the yummy food.

'But look at the chicken I made for you.' I opened the lid and made her smell the delicious curry, hoping she would forgive the mess since I was completely exhausted from my walk and cooking for her and telling my friends I was making dinner for my lovely girlfriend, which had made them call me a wuss.

She was immediately floored. 'Okay I'll clear up later. Let's eat now.'

She spooned the bits of unburnt rice in a bowl, and put some bread on a plate as well. We sat down to eat.

After dinner, I tried to kiss her, but she moved her head to the left and my smooch landed on her ear. 'I still haven't got the gross pictures out of my head, so just take it easy!'

What a waste of a meal. Also, I'd hoped for a second that maybe she was titillated by the videos and would try something new. Unfortunately my clingy girlfriend was a prude.

I'd have to think of a new password for the folder, and quickly get myself an external hard drive. I needed to save my collection before she deleted it. And I now had to hide one more thing from her – when I would watch it! Nope, I wasn't giving up on porn. I was just going to find ways to see it when she wasn't around.

But for now I had saved my relationship and my porn collection.

This note below is for the chicks. Show it to them whenever you are asked about why you need to have a porn stash. I hope that it will help!

Five Reasons Why Men Need Porn

1. Our imagination sucks. Let's face it, we don't have great visualization capacity. That's why we can't read romance novels and get all hot and heavy. We need to see it. It arouses our imaginations. And we are then happy.

2. We don't want to be the odd one out. A man who says he's never watched porn or that he doesn't like it, is seen in the wolf pack as a weirdo. You don't want to be a weirdo. That's like carrying a 'man purse/satchel' as that fat weirdo says in *The Hangover*.

3. Helps us process rejection. When you gals say you're not in the mood, at least we have porn to finish what's started in our head and our bodies. We leave you alone then. Otherwise, the heat could just burn the place down baby.

4. Happy endings. There is so much variety that it never gets boring. If we ask you to try any of those things, you will surely reject us. So while we continue to have normal vanilla sex with you, porn opens up our world to endless possibilities.

5. Daily stress. With high-pressure jobs, cranky bosses, nagging wives, crying babies, never-ending EMIs, a man needs a little pleasure. While he's being the great husband and father at one level, let him get off while watching porn and believing he's the lucky man with a secretary who's dying to give him a BJ.

17

Shubho Mahalaya!

That means the pujos are around the corner. For every Bengali, it is the time of the year when we can go wild. Eating, drinking, dancing and generally making fools of ourselves – it's all allowed for the five days from Maha Shoshti till Dusshami when we immerse the idol. Bongs are allowed to do what they want.

I wasn't going home this year, unfortunately. I hadn't been given leave since a new show was being launched and they needed 'all hands on deck'. Anyway, you can take a Bong out of Kolkata but you can never take pujos out of the Bong. I decided to go pandal-hopping this year in Mumbai and have a blast every day. The smell of shiuli flowers and joss sticks was in the air. Ma Durga was here!

There are about ninety-one pujo pandals in Mumbai. They range from the small ones in gullies to big ones sponsored by rich men who want to atone for their sins. The extremely lavish to the amazingly simple, the celebrity-driven to melodious cultural evenings, the delicious *bhog* to the prettiest idol, I went to all of them. And I dragged Radha with me.

'What will I wear?' she asked. Radha's first reaction to

anything is what will she wear. Even if she had to attend a funeral it would be, 'What do I wear?' Not, 'Oh God, what happened?' Or even, 'Wow, that sounds like fun!' Well, obviously I don't expect her to say that for a funeral, but when we're going pandal-hopping, be a little excited, woman.

'You can wear anything. But let's go soon. I don't want to miss the first *aarti*.'

So from the sixth day, when Ma Durga comes down on earth and the festivities begin, to the last day, Radha and I went for *pushpanjali* in the morning, *bhog* in the afternoon and the *aarti* and cultural festivities in the evening.

To be honest, I didn't have as much fun as I do in Kolkata. Radha constantly cribbed about how hot it was, how boring it was, how she hated to wear a sari and travel on a bike. I tried my best to give her good food at all the places we went. Mukherjee Caterers did an outstanding job of prawn chops. I walloped down some five of them before Radha stopped me. Buzz kill. But I managed to eat about six sandesh at one place and four kala jamuns in another. My stomach hated me for the five days of pujo. But my soul was so happy that it could go on for the rest of the year.

The one thing I couldn't do with Radha around was flirt with all the beautifully-dressed women. Luckily, on Maha Navami, Radha was too tired to go out again (such a non-Bong she is), and I took Menon with me to a pandal. He went completely berserk! He had never seen women wearing such low-cut sari blouses, their hair blow-dried to perfection, big red bindis on their foreheads that said come hither because I'm available. The clinking of bangles on their slender wrists, the soft swaying of their hips as they moved past you seductively to ask for more flowers for the *aarti*. It was all too much for Menon.

'This is like the Navratras but better. The women aren't all sweaty from dancing. They're just these mini goddesses.' Menon ogled and salivated and the women appreciated his glances. Mumbai Bongs are different from Kolkata Bongs. Here women want to be noticed, complimented and admired. In Kolkata, the women have their own groups and only want other women to admire them or be envious of them. The men hardly matter there.

'I told you,' I said as I patted his shoulder. 'Now let's sit and watch the performances.'

We sat in the first row and watched the dances by many children before the real performances began. First several Bengali women danced to some songs, then Sunidhi Chauhan came and belted out some Bollywood numbers and the women danced with their friends around the seating area.

Menon got up to take a picture of them. As an outsider, he began to talk to them about their culture. They were happy to take selfies with him. Which woman doesn't like taking photos when she's dressed up? He was a hit with them because he never went too close but complimented them constantly. He even stood in one corner quietly when the ever-present elderly aunties showed disapproval of their single daughters talking to a man. Honestly, they themselves had met their husbands at a pandal. Not allowing your single adult daughter to meet a man is sheer hypocrisy.

But Menon scored several numbers that night and got invited to an after-pujo party. These are the parties that websites and cultural communities don't talk about. It's like a Filmfare Awards after-party. They take place in different people's houses and the best parties have the coolest crowd, the most amazing booze and the hottest chicks.

I wasn't invited. I had been seen with Radha, who had not met with the approval of this pandal crowd. However Menon pleaded with my community of Bong chicks that I be invited, and they finally relented. I didn't know whether to be thankful or annoyed. But anyway, I couldn't go. Radha missed me, and had sent enough texts accusing me of fooling around with a Bong woman at the pandal. So I rushed back home. Later Menon told me he scored with a Bong woman. And he claimed that the myth was true: they *were* awesome in bed. I don't know how I got stuck with a Punjabi who seemed to have a headache every alternate day.

Five Tips to Ask a Woman Out (Menon's methods)

1. Go solo. Make eye contact with whomever you like. Make sure it's just one girl and your eyes aren't wandering. Smile at her a lot from across the room and make sure she smiles back. Once she does, go over after a while and stand next to her. Compliment her and talk about the ambience. Let her get interested in you.

2. Be casual. Don't talk about serious things. Ask her simple stuff like if the phone she has is a good one since you're planning on switching. Compliment her. Tell her she's so smart. Ask if she would like to grab a coffee somewhere close by. If she wants to bring a friend, agree, but add that she can also just give your number to a friend in case she doesn't want to be alone with you. That way the friend can check up on you, but you have alone time with her.

3. Don't interrupt her. If she's talking to her friends or is with her parents, leave her alone. Stand to one side till she is alone. Then go and speak to her. If she's always surrounded,

ask a waiter to slip her a note. Compliment her in the note – I just wanted to tell you in person how beautiful you look in that red sari but since you're surrounded by family, I thought I would send this note. Forgive me. She'll love you for being a gentleman and keeping your distance.

4. Make the decisions. If you're going to leave it to her to make decisions it'll never happen, so you be the one to do it. But make sure you include her in the decision-making process. Shall we go to a coffee shop or a bar? Friday or Saturday? One in the afternoon good for you? You're most likely to get positive responses than, 'No, I can't make it', 'Where should we go? I have no idea.' If she seems flaky, compliment her. Tell her how you love the softness of her approach and you'll look after all the details. She'll think you're an alpha male and immediately go out with you.

5. Be cool. Finally a woman has agreed to go out with you. Do not start doing jumping jacks. Continue with the conversation. Ask her what she's planned for the rest of the day and say you're looking forward to seeing her. Leave her hoping the date will be great.

Shubho Bijoya!

18

It was a Monday, and I had just reached home, completely tired. Radha was walking in through the gate just as I came up on the bike. She was smiling for a change and I stopped right next to her.

'What's up?' I teased as I came up behind her.

She yelped as she saw me and then burst into a wide smile. 'Look at my mehndi.'

Oh God. I smiled approvingly but completely artificially. See, men don't really care about such things. Mehndi, hair dye, haircuts, new dresses, how fat you're looking, and other such inane things. If you ask us questions about any of the above, you'll get an indifferent answer.

'Pretty,' I said, already blanking out.

'Aren't you going to ask me why I got it?'

I looked at her. That sentence is just loaded for men. No, we don't want to ask, because we don't really care what the answer is. But if it's important to her, then we might as well try to look interested.

So I said the safest thing in my head, 'Sure.'

She giggled and replied, 'It's karva chauth tomorrow. I wanted to keep a fast for you.'

'Karva what?' I asked as I parked my bike in the allocated spot. Someone had thrown some garbage around the area and it made me angry. Why couldn't this society keep its premises clean? The members were so unhygienic. I would definitely tell the landlord that if he wanted to raise the rent, he would have to look after all this nonsense.

In the meantime, Radha was going on about the significance of whatever festival she was celebrating and I nodded along, not really listening. Until she said, 'So I have to fast tomorrow – the whole day.'

'Fast? Like not eat meat?'

She shook her head as we waited for the lift. 'As in not eat or drink anything the whole day.'

I was appalled. Why would anyone do that? I could not imagine any Bengali woman not eating the entire day. She would turn into a praying mantis and eat up the entire household by sunset.

'Radha, why do you want to do this?'

We entered the apartment as she said, 'Well, generally women keep it for men's long lives. Didn't you hear what I was saying earlier?'

I nodded, though of course I hadn't heard a word she'd said. I decided not to ask any more questions.

'Anyway, please come home early tomorrow. I can't eat or drink till I do your puja. And you need to get me a present,' she said as she went and got me a glass of water.

'Present,' I asked with trepidation. 'Why?'

'Because I'm keeping the fast.'

'But I don't want you to keep the fast.' I also didn't want to buy another present. Either it was a gift or it was rent. And I preferred a roof over my head to a silky negligee right

now. Although if it meant her doing things to me outdoors....
My thoughts trailed off.

'Well the mother-in-law has to get a sari but since you
haven't introduced me to your mom, I would expect you to
get something for me.'

Bloody shit. I knew it. Everything was about a present for
the woman. Birthday present, Diwali present, New Year's
present and now karva chauth present. How much can a
man do to get sex. It must be cheaper and more peaceful to
go to a prostitute than be in a committed relationship. Then
there are other complications with that.

I quickly focused again and said, 'Radha, I'm a little short
on cash right now.'

I could see her face become red with anger. 'So you don't
want to get me anything? You cheap bastard. I'm keeping a
fast for you and you can't even buy me something small in
return for my love and prayers for your long life? It's not
about the money. It can be anything as a token of your love.'

I squirmed. 'I....'

'Fine.' She stormed away into the room.

I didn't know what to do, but I followed her in and saw
her sitting on our bed, sulking. I sat on the opposite end and
said, 'How about I keep the fast with you?'

Radha's face softened. 'Really?'

I nodded reluctantly. 'Except I'm going to be at work so I
need to have water at least.'

Radha came up and hugged me, 'Of course. I can tell all
the girls then that my fiancé is keeping a fast for my long life.
Oh how romantic.'

'But will you then forgive me for not getting you a present?'

'Okay, but we'll order in food for dinner.'

I agreed to that. Spending money on food was no problem. At least that was something we both gained from.

The next morning she woke up early to stuff her face with food and water and went back to sleep. I didn't get up. I needed a full eight hours of sleep. So when I woke up I was damn hungry and wanted some eggs for breakfast.

'But darling,' Radha purred, 'you promised you wouldn't eat today.'

Fuck.

'Can I have tea?'

She shook her head.

'Please? I'll die. I won't be able to stay awake at all!'

She finally relented, because after all she was making up all the rules about this stupid tradition that she followed. 'Okay fine. You can have as many cups of tea as you want because this is your first time.'

And last! I wanted to say. Which idiot would do this repeatedly? By next year either I would convince her not to do it, get out of fasting, or get rid of her completely.

I got ready and gulped down two cups of tea and two glasses of water to control my appetite. It didn't help. All I could feel was an empty stomach with liquid swishing around it.

Radha, however, was feeling perfectly fine as she had woken up to eat everything in the fridge. As I was leaving, she said, 'Now remember to keep your promise and get home early so we can eat together. We need to look at the moon before we can eat. I'm going to come back from Bittu di's house by seven. She's having the *katha* there.'

Who the hell was Bittu di? What the hell is a *katha*? But I honestly didn't care as my mood was already turning sour thinking I needed to wait ten-and-a-half hours to eat.

'Okay,' I said and left. I waited for the lift. Then went down and saw there was more garbage around the scooter and bicycle area. I cursed them all. Looked at my watch. Couldn't eat for another ten hours and twenty-three minutes. Fuck.

I honestly believe we need to worship Bheeshma Pitamah from the *Mahabharat*. He made a vow and kept it. Ordinary men cannot keep vows, because life throws you a curve ball just when you least expect it.

When I entered office, everyone seemed happy. Now this was new. Never in my three years of being in this godforsaken place had anyone been really happy. We all came to work because we couldn't find jobs anywhere else. And we tolerated each other because we didn't have friends outside these four walls.

'What's up, dude?' I asked Menon as I got to my desk and placed my helmet in my small cubby hole.

'It's the boss' birthday. He's taking us out for lunch,' Menon said with a wide smile.

'What?' I asked incredulously.

'Ya!' Menon said standing, holding my shoulders and looking in the direction of the boss' cabin. 'Tweedledee is spending company money and taking everyone out for lunch. And not just anywhere. To Mahesh Lunch Home!' Mahesh Lunch Home, to the uninitiated and to the vegans, is food fit for kings, especially for fine connoisseurs of seafood, like me.

The words lunch, buffet, and fish swam in my head. Eat all you want, and not pay for it! And I could have as much fish and prawns as my little Bengali molecules could take. This was the best day ever!

But then I remembered my promise to Radha. *Noooooooooooooo!* I couldn't eat!

I sat down at my desk and held my head, cursing my fate.

'What happened?' Menon asked. 'You're the first person who has had this reaction.'

I looked up at him and said, 'I promised Radha I would fast on karva chauth with her.'

Now friends are supposed to be sympathetic and help each other. But guy friends are really the opposite. Unless there's a free drink in it for them somewhere, they're not really going to sympathize and listen to your troubles.

Menon burst out laughing and said, 'Dude. Your life sucks.' Then he walked away to figure out some work and left me to contemplate my situation.

I decided I would go with the flow. I looked at my watch. It was just nine-thirty. I could probably keep my vow till seven in the evening. I could do this for Radha. I could do it for Bheeshma Pitamah. Nine-thirty two. Who was I kidding? I was already so hungry. And everyone was having breakfast in the canteen.

But I *had* to try. I began working on a presentation with such fervour that I forgot about the time. I downloaded pictures, collected data. Finally I let myself look at my watch. It was just bloody ten o'clock.

I went to the canteen and asked for a cup of tea. I was feeling faint. I needed sugar or I would collapse. Radha hadn't specified how many cups of tea I could have. I suppose I could substitute chai for juice as well. One liquid was the same as another. Wasn't it?

So I had three cups of tea and two glasses of juices and felt a bit better. I passed an hour faffing with the marketing team, discussing a few ideas on how to promote shows using bikini waxes as the new in-thing, and feeling like I could keep my promise to Radha.

Before I knew it, it was noon. The boss walked out of his cabin and called out to me. 'Obro! You can come with me. Everyone, let's leave so we don't get caught in traffic.'

There was a loud cheer and Menon looked at me with a smile. 'You're riding with the boss! What an honour!'

I knew that any excuse to stay in office wouldn't work. I was *forced* to head out for lunch. It was destiny. It was pulling me. I couldn't do anything about it. This was totally going with the flow. The boss got into his car and made a call to his wife, 'Yes darling, I'm taking the team out for dinner today since I'm in meetings the whole day. You don't believe me, you can ask Obro. He's with me for my meetings right now.' Tweedledee handed me the phone, told me to speak to his wife, and gave me a look as if to say I needed to go with the flow of his lies.

'Yes ma'am, I'm Obrokranti Banerjee. I'm with Sir. We have meetings the whole day.' I handed the phone back to my boss.

'I'll be late then, Swaty,' he said. 'Don't wait up.'

He hung up and then made another call. 'Hello darling. Yes I'll be there as soon as I leave these people at Mahesh. You check in. I'll come and have lunch with you.'

So, my boss wanted me as a foil for his infidelities. He didn't really care what my opinion was on marketing strategy. And he picked me because I didn't have the balls to tell anyone else. What a genius he was. I had more respect for him than ever before. I needed to learn the ways of two-timing women from him. If I stuck around close enough, I would figure out how to keep Radha *and* cheat on her. What a wonderful thought.

When we reached Mahesh Lunch Home, there was a

buffet set up just for our office and everyone grabbed a plate and heaped food on it immediately. I felt dejected. The aroma of prawns butter pepper garlic and fish Malabari wafted in my direction as I ordered a nimbu paani.

Menon looked at me and said, 'Just eat, man. This opportunity doesn't come often. There'll be karva chauth next year as well. She'll never know.'

I agreed. I grabbed a plate and put butter garlic prawns, tandoori fish, chicken Malabar gravy and mutton roganjosh on it. I got a separate plate for rice and four butter naans. I was going to have a food orgy. And I wouldn't need to tell Radha at all. What she didn't know wouldn't hurt her. Unfortunately, what I didn't see would hurt me later.

19

After the lunch, I got stuck in office with some work that the boss had given me while he traipsed off with his girlfriend. It was way past sunset when I got a call from Radha.

'Where are you?' she demanded sternly. I shat my pants as I remembered it was karva chauth and she had kept a fast for me. And supposedly I had kept one for her as well.

'I'm just leaving,' I said hurriedly as I switched off my laptop and gathered my things.

'It's eight o' clock! You should have been here by now! It will take you an hour or more to reach home!' she shouted at the other end of the phone while I ran out the office door. I have no idea why women want to keep this dumb fast. There are other ways to show us you love us. I can think of a few Kamasutra positions women could try out that would make us extremely happy. But keeping a fast, and then getting cranky because you've had no water or food because of me when I haven't even asked you to do it is just wrong.

It did take more than an hour to reach home, but thankfully it was a precious few moments before the moon was spotted.

When I reached home, Radha was on the rooftop of the

building with other women. As soon as I saw her, my jaw dropped in amazement. A flood of emotions swept through me. She was dressed in bridal finery. If she were a bride. She was wearing a bright pink and orange sari, a chiffon pink dupatta draped on her head, jewellery on her neck and ears, and a teeka on her forehead. She'd adorned her wrists with many bangles that tinkled away when she moved towards me. With the mehndi on her feet and hands all the way up to her elbows, I felt like I was in a Yash Raj movie. I dropped my bag, put one foot behind the other, and opened my arms like Shah Rukh so she could race into them. She snapped her fingers and asked me to join her. There would be no running in her heels.

As I swaggered towards her, I thought how seductive it would be for her to be sitting demurely without saying a word on a decorated bed as I removed the dupatta and her clothes. Very Hindi filmy types. Music in the background. Smell of jasmine flowers in her hair. Wow!

Then suddenly I wondered where she'd got all these clothes and how much money she'd spent on them. Was she stealing money from my wallet? A memory flash hit me as I remembered how she'd taken five hundred rupees for a packet of milk once and then didn't give me back the change. Maybe she had been pilfering money from me on the side to buy herself things!

'There's the moon!' a child said, pointing it out to his mother. Radha came to me and smiled.

'How do I look?'

'Beautiful, Radha. Simply ravishing. Where did you...' My voice trailed off as she looked at the moon through a sieve that I had never seen before and did some aarti to me and the moon. I liked this. I was being worshipped as a God. I could get used to this. If only she worshipped me at home in ordinary clothes as well.

Then I fed her a sweet and some water. A woman who was a widow but overseeing the entire function for the society came up to us and said, 'Oh you're Obrokranti? Radha was saying you kept a fast for her as well. How sweet of you. May you have a long and happy married life.'

Yikes! Married? That was a bit much. 'Radha what have you told them?' I said, panicked. If my mother found out, I would be dead.

Radha only put a hand to her lips and said, 'Shhh. I couldn't say we were living together. No one accepts women who do that. Now here, eat this, you must be...wait...what's that on your shirt?'

She looked closer at my shirt and realized at the same time that there was a food stain on it. Crap. I must have dropped something at Mahesh Lunch Home.

'One of the guys bumped into me at lunch. Probably something fell.'

She looked closer and saw there were two distinct stains. One from a red curry. And one near my stomach, which was yellow. She looked at me sternly and asked, 'Did you eat something?'

Bengalis have this characteristic that no one else does. They're dumb with lies. They *think* they can lie well, but they always get caught because it shows on their faces. That's why they don't make good businessmen and they can never win at *taash*. Everyone knows when they're bluffing.

'Absolutely not!' I tried to say earnestly. 'I have not!'

She glared at me and hissed, 'Tell me the truth!'

I looked down in embarrassment and said, 'The boss took us out for the first time in three years and that too to Mahesh Lunch Home.' As if mentioning Mahesh Lunch Home would save the day.

Radha's face became more red than the bangles on her wrist. I looked at her sheepishly and noticed vermillion in her hair. 'Did you put sindoor?' I asked.

'Shut up!' she said and stormed away from me. I quickly followed her, not wanting to upset her any further. And more importantly not wanting to get locked out of my house again and spend a night on the doorstep.

'Radha, listen to me,' I said as we got into the lift, but she just turned away.

In the house, she banged the thali on the dining table, walked to the kitchen and put a pot of water to boil. I thought she wanted to throw it at me so I began to ramble desperately.

'I'm so sorry Radha. I should have just listened...'

But Radha wouldn't hear any of it. She started speaking and didn't stop till the water had boiled and nearly evaporated. 'I did this puja for you. I didn't have water even. And you were stuffing your face at Mahesh. Why couldn't you wait till tomorrow? No I don't want to hear your boss took you. You can't go yourself? One thing you said you will do for me and you didn't do it. What do you do for me in any case?'

I started to say, 'I pay for the groceries, the electricity, for this house where you stay for free–'

'Free?' she screamed, 'You think I stay for free? I manage your house. I look after your laundry, your food, and you. I'm the one who holds your life together and this is how you repay me? You can't even keep a fast.'

Honestly I had several things to say in my mind, but I realized that the only one that was going to work was if I praised her. 'Darling you look so beautiful today. I've never seen you look this gorgeous.'

'Shut up!' she said.

Obviously, that angle wasn't going to work either. I looked down and felt terribly sorry for all the food I had. It was now churning in my stomach. In fact, I had to go to the loo.

As I walked towards the bathroom, Radha said, 'Where do you think you're going? I'm not done yet.'

'Can you hold that thought. I really need to go dump,' I said in the most frank manner possible.

'If you hadn't eaten so much, maybe you wouldn't have to go!'

Well I had. And now I could hear it rumbling in my stomach. Radha went on and on speaking and soon enough I had to push her aside and rush to the bathroom where within moments of me pulling my pants down, all the contents from the lunch came out. What a relief.

But when I went out to hear her lecture again, I saw that she was now seething and crying. 'You shouldn't have pushed me!'

I went to hold her, 'Darling I didn't. You just were blocking the entrance. I would have shat in my pants if you hadn't moved.'

'So it's my fault?' she shouted again as I reeled back.

'No it's mine. As usual,' I sighed. I realized that one could never win in relationships. Men always needed to take the blame and give the credit. Only then could it be called equality for women. I said, 'How about I make you a cup of tea and take you out for a lovely dinner – wherever you want to go.'

At the thought of food and a hot cup of tea, Radha became quiet. Before she could say anything further, I made her a cup of tea and handed her biscuits. I started playing with her hair. 'How pretty your hair is looking.'

'Now don't start Obro!' she said, snapping. 'I know what's on your mind.'

Heck. It's always on my mind. But today, to deflower a virginal-looking bride would be special. I guess this is why women keep karva chauth. So men are reminded of the wedding day when the woman was submissive, demure and shy. It keeps them going for all other three hundred and sixty-four days when she becomes a *jandrel* – wild animal.

'Where's my present?' Radha asked as she finished her tea.

'I thought we were only going out for dinner?' I said, reminding her of our promise.

'That was when you were supposed to be fasting as well.'

'Well, we'll go anywhere you want. And you can eat whatever you like. No ordering in tonight.' I felt magnanimous. I wanted to prove to her that I loved her. So what if I hadn't fasted, she was still the love of my life. I had to show her that I cared about her. A fast couldn't be the test of love. It has to come from everyday actions. One day can't determine how you feel about the person in your life. That's why I hated Valentine's Day and birthdays and karva chauth. They were tests for all of us. As if how we lived every other day, giving respect, love and understanding didn't matter.

I took Radha out that evening and spent a bomb on our dinner. A week later she swiped my debit card for a new sari. There really is no justice in this world. And men will remain suckers for the love of their lives.

But I did get to unwrap that sari. And I truly understood why men got married. For that one night. That moment. The realization that you have a demure bride on your bed. You feel like the king of the world!

Five Ways to Be a Good Lover

1. Go slow. Romance is the key word. There's no hurry. Remove clothes slowly. Kiss passionately followed by slowly. Look deep into her eyes. You need not always be touching and becoming fiery in bed. Stroke gently. Speak softly to her about how beautiful she is.

2. Comfort is key. Make sure she's comfortable with the AC, the surroundings. You might want to ravage her on the kitchen counter, but if she's in pain, she's not going to be happy. Check if she's okay. If she's going with the flow, let it be.

3. Massage her. Shoulders, neck, lower back, arms and finally her secret garden. Use your fingers gently. About a millimetre above her skin. You're not a Thai specialist and you don't need to knead her knots away. You need to arouse her. Ask her if she's liking it. Don't rush it till she's ready. Use your thumb and middle finger to rub her softly. Gradually increase the pace.

4. Kissing. Soft kisses around her body and her erogenous zones arouses a woman. Spiral your tongue in certain places. It drives women wild.

5. Loving. During the act, don't say dirty things that will turn her off, unless she wants you to. Be aware of whether she's in the moment. Try not to climax before her. You'll know she's done when her face is relaxed.

Enjoy yourself!

20

The dinner and the sari must have finally made Radha a little happy, because a couple of days later, she came bounding up to me and said, 'Why don't you call your friends over on Friday night to our place? I will cook some nice mutton and chicken starters, you buy booze for them and just relax with them over Friday night till Saturday afternoon. I can go across and stay with Kaki.'

I stopped whatever I was doing (which was staring vacantly in space) and literally fell to the ground off the diwan. What! JOY! I wanted to smooch her. She seemed to be floating in an ethereal way, almost like an angel in pink, singing paeans to a TBNO!

The most sacred of sacred nights is The Boys Night Out (TBNO). It is a night of revelry, much drinking, some singing, some dancing, lots of bitching (about bosses, girlfriends, and the likes), reminiscing, puking, card games, more drinking and more puking. In short, you feel like you are 'the king of the world', you are the Batman, you are Mark Zuckerberg (if you're the geeky type) or whatever.

TBNO defines you, makes you feel alive. Makes you feel non-alone, aligned to others, bonding with your buddies.

Drinking and lots of drinking is possible only with true friends. Especially since the next morning, you should be able to face your good friend and smile at the memory of calling him a dog fucker to his face. Actually bitch fucker or some such canine bullshit. In addition, he shouldn't be trying to strangle you at the same happy thought.

I couldn't believe she was allowing me to have a night exclusively for myself with my guy friends. Was she the coolest girlfriend ever? This would make up for all the times my friends had excluded me. Once I invited them over, I would be back in their good books and have several nights out with the boys again.

I said a reverential 'thank you' to Radha and almost cried afterwards with happiness. Finally, composing myself, I started texting all my office friends and some college friends about this coming joyful Friday. I asked her, 'How many joyful friends can I call?' She said 'What?' I said, 'I meant how many people?' She asked me to decide and just tell her so she could cook accordingly.

The week passed quickly, even before I could say 'Quikr' (not paid plug), and soon it was the night of TBNO! Half the colleagues invited were coming straight from office with me and they manfully bought their own booze at the first wine shop we saw. Obviously, we also bought a few pints for the long drive back home, which we finished off in the cab. Menon also offered a pint to the cab driver, sharing his joy with the world at large. Thankfully, the cab driver refused and we had an uneventful drive back home. We also picked up chaknas, some fiery wasabi nuts to munch on, and finally reached our destination. My place. Radha was dressed to thrill and had finished all her cooking by then.

The boys sat down in the front hall and pulled out their packs of cigarettes, as I hastily assembled make-shift ashtrays. Radha said she would have one drink, and so the boys, exhibiting maximum male chivalry, poured her a lemony vodka drink. The boys started to unwind, and soon the rest of the guys trooped in. It was around eight o'clock now; I looked at Radha questioningly (as to when she was leaving for her kaki's place). She looked at me steadily and said, 'Ya sure, I will have just one more drink.'

And then.

She sat through the entire TBNO. Fucking hell, yeah. The poor boys felt so intimidated, the conversation was muted and polite. Some of them actually spoke about a bloke called Murakami, and how well he told stories about cats. See, the thing is this. Boys will always not be boys in front of intimidating girlfriends. They suddenly become polite people, mindful of their language, their posture, how much they're drinking. So no slurring happens, no falling down on the floor, no dares, no gallis and no puking. In short, we could have been drinking at an official dinner at the Library Bar. The entire point of TBNO was suddenly and surely lost.

After some five-odd drinks, Srini, a colleague, commented that his mother was waiting for him back home with some curd rice and he needed to go. Surprisingly, everyone remembered their mothers, girlfriends, dogs, bosses and said urgent errands awaited them, and soon it was a quick dinner and the boys left at a very early eleven-thirty, instead of the wee hours of dawn.

'That was fun,' Radha said after they had left and she was finishing her fourth drink. Right.

It was the most lousy TBNO. Ever. In the period of

mankind. Bitter. Bitter. Bitter. And no matter what I did afterwards, no one ever came back to my place. Everyone had some excuse or another. And Radha would often say, 'Let's go partying with your guy friends. Haven't caught up with them for ages!'

21

My mother had stopped speaking to me because I hadn't been able to go home for the pujos. But my organization had not been willing to give me leave. Besides, Radha would have wanted to come and I didn't know if I wanted to introduce her to my family just yet. Radha was sweet, loving, and extremely warm when she wanted to be. But when she was possessive, she became a tigress. I didn't know how she would react with all the pampering my mother and cousin Nandini would shower me with. And I doubted if she would let me hang out with my friends alone.

But now, with Diwali around the corner, I was thinking again of going to Kolkata. Lengtu really wanted to see me. He had become serious about a girl and he wanted my opinion of her before he told the family. That was quite an honour because he never asked for my opinion. I didn't know how to ask for leave from my boss, but first I had to take leave from Radha.

I broached the subject tenderly to Radha. We were downstairs, slowly walking around the apartment complex as part of our evening exercise.

'Radha,' I started, 'what are your plans for Diwali? Do you want to visit your family?'

Radha squealed with joy and said, 'That's such a great idea. We can travel to Pune and you can meet my family and we can officially tell them we're getting married next December.'

What the...

'Whoa! Where did that come from, Radha?' I asked.

'Don't you want to get married?'

'Radha, I was talking about us going back to our respective families to celebrate Diwali. I haven't seen my parents for over a year and Shubir needed some brotherly advice from me. I am the only one they rely on. I am the fulcrum on which the family pivots. I'm indispensable to them. And now they need me. It's my duty to go back and meet them.'

Radha was quiet, trying to assimilate how important I was to my family as well as her. 'Then I'll come with you.'

I had known this would come and I was prepared. 'But I think we need to set the base to tell our families about each other. And once they want to meet us, we can travel together to Pune and Kolkata and make our engagement official. We can't just spring ourselves on each other's families. They will be shocked and reject the whole thing.'

Radha understood. She nodded and kept quiet. Then she had a thought, 'But then I need to know where you are at all times. How do I know you won't go out with some random woman?'

I laughed. I knew I was irresistible, but I didn't know she was so insecure about me. 'Don't worry about that. I will ward off all the women who want to be with me.'

'How?'

'How?' I asked back.

'Ya, how?' she asked again and this time folded her arms and looked at me straight in the eye.

'I don't know.' I was honestly stumped.

'I do. We put rings on each other.'

What the...

'Excuse me?' I asked, feigning ignorance.

'We officially get engaged. We buy rings and put them on each other. Have a small ceremony at home.'

My super-brain had to think quickly. Getting engaged would mean several questions from family and friends. I didn't know if I was ready for that. 'How much will it cost? Wouldn't we want our families involved? Don't you want to wait till we're sure our families like each other?'

But Radha would have none of it. So that afternoon, for the first time in my life, I was dragged to a jewellery shop where we sat and discussed ring sizes and diamond quality.

'What do you have for five thousand rupees? For both?' I asked boldly.

Radha gave me a dirty glare and looked through me. She took a sip of the complimentary ice tea they had served and I asked for four more glasses of it. I was going to get my money's worth for this goddamn ring. Until I had to rush to the bathroom twice in half an hour. What was with the AC in this place anyway.

The shop owner showed her many rings and everything was worth more than the bike I had. The ring she picked out was over a lakh, and she argued with him to show her a downsized version. But he said that all solitaire diamonds were expensive.

I leaned in and whispered in her ear, 'Radha, I cannot afford anything this expensive yet.'

She shooed me away. Dejected, I looked away. A pretty, petite sales woman next to the bangle counter smiled at me.

I suddenly thought to myself, 'What would Lengtu do to get out of a tricky situation?' Suddenly I had a plan in my head.

I shrugged and muttered loud enough for Radha to hear, 'Well if you're not interested in anything I have to say...'

I casually walked over to the girl at the bangle counter and said, 'Can I see those bangles?' She took them out and showed them to me. I could see Radha looking at me suspiciously. I smiled sweetly at the sales woman and said, 'I would like to see them on you.'

I could see Radha seething. The woman wore them and I gently took her wrist and examined the bangles. 'Very pretty.'

Radha left the ring section and came to stand with her hands on her hips near the counter, 'What are you doing?'

'Nothing.'

'You can't afford these bangles.'

'I can't afford anything in this store. But that hasn't stopped you from wasting my time here. So I thought I might as well hang out with Sulaksha here.'

Radha's face burned red. 'Get up. We're leaving.'

She turned and walked away and I smiled politely at the sales people and thanked them for their time. Mission accomplished. I got Radha out of the store and I didn't have to spend any money! The best way to get out of any tricky predicament is to divert a woman's attention. At least for a few moments you'll be safe. You'll obviously still have problems later, but for a little time you can rest happy you're out of the sticky situation. And jealousy is the mother of all tricks. Women would rather have you in their life than any of the other things.

You see, a man is a woman's greatest possession. She has moulded a man according to her needs. She has spent time on him. Trained him to understand her, come home to her, and obey her. She has invested emotionally, mentally and physically in that relationship. She will not walk out easily unless you do something stupid and violent. Then she'll take everything you have and walk out, and you end up in jail. But until then, she will only be upset that you haven't 'understood' her.

So here's the thing. Most men understand that they will be moulded and trained. They get the woman very early on. They like being putty in the woman's hands, but when it comes to using it against her, we're the masters babe! We know just when to get you upset enough to move away from that situation and train us 'all over again'.

Radha didn't speak to me all the way home on the bike. Probably because I wore a helmet that was extra padded to obliterate outside noise like a pillion rider. I smiled smugly. I felt like Muhammad Ali after he won the World Heavyweight Championship. 'Float like a butterfly, sting like a bee.' That was me!

When we got home, Radha demanded to know what I was doing with that 'other woman'.

'Honey, I was just looking at bangles I thought would like nice on you,' I said sweetly.

'You were flirting with that woman!'

I shrugged and said, 'Why would I do that? I know you don't like it.'

Radha went into the kitchen to make some tea and I followed her.

'Radha,' I said gingerly, 'I'm not making enough money to afford rings or an engagement. I'm barely making anything to keep us afloat here. So either you find a job and pool in, or you try and understand that all these expenses are going to leave me broke and without money to even pay for a roof over our heads.'

Radha was sullen and silent for some time. 'No one has asked me to find a job before. With the class of family I come from, we don't find jobs. We have a business. And we don't serve people!'

The water had started boiling and I was hoping that Radha would make me some tea. But she just stood there glaring at me. So once again, I made tea for both of us. I hadn't trained this woman at all. Ooff.

'Well then why don't you ask your family to lend you some money? Then you can buy all the things I can't afford.'

I took my cup of tea, walked to the drawing room, and put on the television. Radha followed with her cup and sat next to me, 'I can't ask them for money. They expect me to find a nice boy who can provide for me. Otherwise they'll get me married off to another businessman's son. And I refuse to have an arranged marriage. It's against my principles. I want to have a love marriage. That's why I fell in love with you!'

'Radha, my darling, I love you too,' I said, 'but until I can bring in a fat salary, you'll have to suppress your desires for anything but my body. Only that I can give to you free.'

Radha laughed and gave me a fat kiss on my lips. And slowly she started unbuttoning my shirt. This day was going to end well after all! She wanted to prove how much she loved me and what I would lose if I left her for Sulaksha the saleswoman. The plan of mine had worked in myriad ways and today was the best day of my life!

22

Finally, it turned out that I couldn't take a break for Diwali. My boss Tweedledee decided to take me on a business trip to Delhi around the same time. Radha was most upset. She couldn't believe that I would be away from her for two whole days. The night before I left she handed me two batteries.

'What's this?' I asked, taking them.

'Two extra batteries for your phone. They're both charged. So if one dies, you can put in the other and when you get the chance, you can recharge all of them. That way I can reach you at all times.'

The woman didn't give me any breathing space! 'How can I be available at all times? What if I'm in a meeting?'

'Then you can pick up and tell me you're in a meeting. But you always need to pick up. You know the rules, Obro. Stop asking me as if this were the first time you need to answer my call. I'm the most important person in your life and you'd better pick up when I call.'

I conceded. I didn't want to argue about small little things. Through the course of the morning, just before we took off, I sent Radha fifteen messages and called her twelve times reassuring her that I wasn't going on a holiday with another woman. She warned me not to switch off my phone until the plane was just taking off. So when we hit the runway, I called and whispered, 'Radha, we're taking off now. I need to switch off my phone.' The airhostess and the passenger next to me gave me dirty looks and I quickly switched off my phone. There were three flights ahead of us in the queue for take-off and it took ten minutes extra before we left. As soon we landed and I was allowed to switch my phone back on, Radha called and screamed, 'You were in the bathroom with an airhostess weren't you? I knew you would cheat on me!'

While I tried to calm her down, my co passengers giggled at my situation. Radha raved and ranted all the way till I got my luggage out. 'Why did the flight take two hours and ten minutes and not two hours as you had told me? Either you're lying to me about the time or the slutty airhostess. Which one is it?'

I finally found Tweedledee – who had travelled business class. He snapped his fingers at me and I told Radha that my boss needed me and I had to hang up. She only agreed after I'd held up the phone near him while he shouted instructions to the porter handling his luggage, just to prove I was with him.

We reached the hotel and Tweedledee went to a suite while I checked in to a smaller room that was clean and nice. It had HD TV and a mini bar. I was set. Then Tweedledee called me on my phone and asked to come to his suite. When I went I saw a woman there, making herself comfortable on the bed, and I realized that I was a decoy.

'Obro,' Tweedledee started, 'take my phone and if Swaty calls, please tell her I'm in a meeting. I've told her you've come on this business trip with me. And if she insists on talking to me, message me from your phone on this other number I have and I'll give you further instructions.'

'Yes sir. When are we going to the conference, sir?' I asked innocently.

'Aah yes. You need to prepare a presentation for the conference tomorrow, on the marketing strategies we're putting together for the coming year. I hope you've brought your laptop.'

With that, he slammed the door shut on my face, leaving me with his phone and a growing anxiety. I looked down and saw that his wife was calling. I answered, saying, 'Hello ma'am, this is Obrokranti Banerjee.'

She remembered who I was and told me to ask her husband to call back. I thought of ringing the doorbell to Tweedledee's suite since I was still standing outside but I could hear activities being carried on inside that if disturbed would probably lead to me getting fired. Honestly I don't know why people don't put on the TV while doing what they need to do in hotel rooms. At least be considerate of your neighbours who aren't having as great a time as you. You don't expect them to smoke a cigarette afterwards since your sex was obviously so great and loud.

I mean, they've come with their children. There isn't much they can do.

'I'll tell him to call you back, ma'am. The conference has just begun and he's asked not to be disturbed.'

I went back to my room and switched on my laptop. Luckily there was free wi-fi. I cracked open a beer from the mini bar and a bag of peanuts and sat down to work. Just then Radha called. 'Hello honey. I'm missing you.'

'Where the fuck are you? I was calling your room to check if you're there but the operator said there was no answer? Who were you fucking?'

Jesus. Here we go again. 'Did you not think that I might be in my boss' room?'

'Yes. And I asked them to connect me there, but the operator said it had a do-not-disturb sign on it. And why would you and your boss have that unless this is revealing a side of you I did not know, Obrokranti!'

'Jesus Radha, you think I'm gay now?'

'I don't know what to think. Why don't you start by telling me the truth?'

Finally I told her I had plenty of work for tomorrow, and that I needed to hang up. But just then, she caught me chugging on my beer. Burp!

'Are you telling me you're drinking while you're working?'

Fuck. I was caught.

'I'm having tea. Now I have to go.'

'Fine. I'll call you every half hour on your landline. And you had better pick up or else!'

Radha cut the call just as the boss' wife called on his phone. 'Obro can you please ask my husband to call me back? I need to ask him something.'

'Sure. I will ask him to call you as soon as there's a lunch break, ma'am.'

'Thank you. And don't call me ma'am. Just call me Swaty.'

I sent a message immediately from my phone to the boss' Delhi number but there was no reply. Promptly, after half an hour, Radha's call came to check if I was working. I had ordered food by then and room service brought me a club sandwich with extra chicken and ham. I ate while speaking to Radha about what was happening back in Mumbai. And then I told her I had to get back to work.

Tweedledee's wife called a few times and started sounding suspicious. I desperately tried to send messages to the dumb ass boss but he refused to answer.

I fell asleep in the afternoon and Radha called. I shouted at her for not letting me sleep or trusting me. She left me alone for exactly one hour while I caught an afternoon nap. By the time I woke up the sun was setting and I hadn't even started the presentation. I decided to take a walk by the pool to refresh myself a bit. I walked around the gorgeous property and had tea by the poolside. I felt like I was on vacation. Never had I stayed anywhere so lavish and luxurious.

Unfortunately, I forgot to take the phones with me downstairs, and by the time I got back to my room, the boss' wife and my girlfriend had left several messages for me. Just then one of the cell phones rang. I picked up and said, 'Swaty, I'm so sorry I missed your calls.'

'I knew it! Who the hell is Swaty?' Radha shouted.

'Radha! It's you!'

'Of course it's me. And now I know you're cheating on me. Who the hell is Swaty? I knew you were screwing another woman! I can't believe you would cheat on me. After all I've done for you. This is how you repay my love.' She started sobbing on the phone and before I could explain myself the other phone started ringing.

I couldn't ignore my boss' wife's call, so I picked up and said, 'I'm so sorry, Swaty. By mistake I gave my phone to your husband.'

'You're having an affair with a married woman?' Radha shouted on the other line.

I quickly whispered into my phone, 'Radha, I can't talk right now.' I hung up and decided that it was time to disturb the boss. I rushed to his room. 'Your wife called ten times sir,' I said when he opened the door.

'Fool,' he yelled at me. 'Why didn't you tell me?'

'I tried, sir. I sent you many messages.'

He looked at his phone which showed that he hadn't got a single message. Apparently I'd been sending messages saying 'your wife is calling' to a wrong number. Later on, that wrong number, a woman, called to ask which wife I was talking about. It was all a horrible misunderstanding.

Tweedledee made up with his wife and had a splendid day with his girlfriend. But I was nowhere close to being free from Radha or the presentation that was due the next day. The lavish vacation had just turned into a terrible headache.

23

Tweedledee and I returned to Mumbai the very next day. Some emergency at home made him cancel his plans. But I stayed on for a little longer that day to attend the conference in the hotel banquet hall. It was the most boring thing I had ever done, but the buffet was great and I met new people and smoked as many cigarettes as I wanted.

Before he left, Tweedledee told me I had better be more careful the next time. I was thrilled there would be a next time. He even promised to give me a Diwali bonus for all my efforts. I was so thrilled. This meant I could finally buy the new Xbox! Not only had the company paid for all my room service, I was also getting a full Diwali bonus. And I'd had alone time away from Radha. It had given me perspective. I realized that Radha wasn't the right woman for me. Now that I would be earning more and was going to be the boss' right-hand man, I needed to be more free and independent. The pressure of being with Radha was getting to me. I decided to cut her off. I would break up with her. I just didn't know how to do it.

When I returned to office, I decided Menon would be the right person to help.

'You gotta leave the country, man,' he said.

So I decided he would not be the right person to help. Obviously he hadn't had many good break-ups. He was thirty-four and still single. Either he had to get his act together really soon or he would be happily single for the rest of his life.

I decided to do it the normal way. I would deny her sex. Use the same tactic she did on me.

When I went back home, Radha was watching TV. I slowly stripped off my shirt in front of her.

'Can you please put that in the washing machine? And move. You're blocking my view of the TV.'

Well, obviously that hadn't worked. I decided to speak to Nandini so Radha would get jealous. When I tried to call my cousin, she didn't pick up. Bummer. Nothing was going right. I walked into the bedroom and the window was open. There was a cool draft of air that wafted in. It felt like Antarctica suddenly.

I needed to get something warm to wear immediately. I called out to Radha. 'Where have you kept my monkey cap?'

Radha didn't respond. I opened my cupboard and stared at it for a really long time. One whole minute. And then I asked her again, 'Radha, have you kept my woollens somewhere?'

'What is wrong with you?' she finally said. 'It's thirty-three degrees outside.'

'Yes, but there's a cold breeze blowing. I need my sweater.'

Radha didn't respond. Damn that TV show. It probably had Shah Rukh Khan doing sit-ups. No woman would move if that were ever on.

So I opened the box under the bed and took out everything

from inside it. I still couldn't find my woollens. And the breeze had made the room so cold.

Now here's a thing about Bengalis that no one knows. We're tropical people. No doctor has been able to figure out why the Bengali race is as susceptible to the cold as Raina is to the short ball. We catch a cold very easily. That's why we will always remember our mother's first words to us: '*Thanda lege jabe.*' (You will catch a cold.) Hence the need to bundle up and wear something warm at the hint of coolness in the air. My grandmother used to say the first chill of winter is '*praanghati*' – deadly. 'Season change *hoche.*' With the changing of the weather, we need to stock up on cough syrups, Crocin and D Cold tablets. That's why, when there's a cool breeze blowing, you'll find a Bengali wearing gear that resembles an Arctic explorer's. Pullovers, mufflers, monkey caps, gloves and thick woollen socks are a must in every Bong man's wardrobe. Which is why it was irritating me that I couldn't find what I was looking for. Already, I could feel a scratch in my throat.

And my girlfriend wasn't helping me or sympathizing with my state at all.

'Radha!' I screamed one last time for the impossible woman. She had overtaken my house and hidden all my essential belongings. I rummaged through her drawers and all the cupboards, throwing things everywhere so the cold wouldn't catch me before I found my monkey cap.

Radha walked in and saw the room. 'What a mess, Obro!'

Honestly I don't know why women state the obvious. Yes the room is a mess. But whose fault is that? If she had just come to help me find what I wanted, I would not have gone rummaging through all the things that are hidden in boxes.

'What do you want?' she asked.

'My muffler, sweater and monkey cap, to begin with.'

She turned and opened a drawer in the dresser near the bathroom wall. She took out a sweater, muffler and monkey cap and gave it to me. 'Honestly, I don't know why you don't know where all your things are. You also live in this house.' And she turned and went back to watching TV.

Well if she didn't put away all my things and just left them in plain clear sight I would know where they were then, na? How am I supposed to find anything if it's neatly tucked away in dressers and cupboards. Men are not supposed to look for things. If they're not in sight, they're hidden. A bachelor pad has no need for cupboards or drawers. Every paper he needs will be on the floor and every item of clothing on the bed. IN PLAIN SIGHT. Where we can find it.

Anyway I left everything on the bed, wore my sweater and went outside.

Instead of commiserating with me because I was freezing my ass off, she started laughing. I grumbled, 'I've come home. It's so cold. You can't even give me tea.'

She went to the kitchen and I called out, 'Forget tea. *Iktu* Horlicks *dao*. Give me some Horlicks and hot milk.'

I needed to keep my immunity up. Nobody knows this but Horlicks is the reason why Bengalis are super strong. We are fed this from the time of birth until we die. I can remember my grandfather at the age of ninety-two asking for Horlicks on his deathbed, hoping it would extend his life by a few more years. It's a miracle potion that can give you immense strength.

Horlicks is also what increases a Bengali man's libido.

Believe it or not, most men have a glass just before they retire for the night so they can go all night long if they have to. That's what makes us so awesome.

Radha came back with tea.

The woman just didn't get me. I needed to break up with her.

I drank the tea. Well obviously. I didn't want it poured over my head. And then I spoke to her. 'Radha, do you think we make a good couple?' I wanted her to say she needed a break from me. Then it would be her decision to break up. I would look like the good guy in the situation and be set scot free from guilt or blackmail.

'Yes. We make a cute couple. I complement you very well.'

Crap. And what the fuck! I was the better looking one. I could look good with anyone. Even make Sunny Leone look sexier. Ha!

I thought of another strategy. 'But do you think we're truly happy together?'

'I think you can try a little harder to make me happy. But don't worry, I can teach you how.'

What the...

A man is not a dog that needs to be taught. Either we make you happy or we don't. And if we don't then don't be with us, goddammit.

But Radha wasn't getting the point. Clearly she didn't see that this relationship wasn't working. I had to tell her in another way. 'Radha,' I started, but forgot the words as Sourav Ganguly came on screen. He was hosting *Kaun Banega Crorepati* in Bengali! I had to watch this program. It was an amazing show. I could break up with Radha tomorrow.

How did one more day matter? At least I could see Dada on screen. How much I missed his batting. Every Bengali has a special connection with him. He made all Bengalis proud.

'Karl Marx,' I shouted the answer to a question he asked the contestant. '*Kamon* Bangali. Karl Marx *ke jaano na?*' I was getting more and more upset with the contestant who was taking his time to answer a simple question that even a fifth grader in Bengal would know.

Radha got up and set the table for dinner. She had made some fish curry and rice for a change. What a sweet thing to do. She didn't even change the channel when the contestant got the answer wrong. She knew I wanted to see the show with Sourav.

I wondered for just a brief second why she was behaving so nicely. I would know soon enough the plan up her sleeve. And then I would never be able to break up with her!

24

'Dada *ki* party *koren!*' Lengtu said on the phone to me. We were discussing my boss who had a woman at home and a woman in a hotel at all times. Earlier, the phrase meant Bengalis who would discuss Marxism and Lenin under a thick smoke of cigarettes in their favourite *adda* while drinking pots of chai. Then in the '80s and '90s the phrase shifted to the Communist Party of India and whether you were 'in' or 'out' of their policymaking. Nowadays it meant general debauchery on another level.

'That's the way I want to be married. At least have two women in my life. The bloody society has stopped polygamy. I can't be committed to one girl for the rest of my life. Shiuli wants to get married. And the parents have agreed. Even the horoscopes match. *Ki korbo?*' Apparently Lengtu was getting cold feet. It must mean he was truly in love. Because obviously men who are really in love run from their feelings and the girl instead of facing them. It's a biological thing that no science has been able to explain.

'Lengtu, get your head together. *Iktu* Black Dog *khao. Shob theek hoye jabe.*' Men can't really give advice to other men, apart from telling them to go ahead and have a drink to forget their problems. Maybe I should just put him on to Menon.

I was so pleased that Radha and I hadn't reached the never-going-back stage. That's one of the four stages of a relationship for a man.

1. Can I Have Sex With You Stage: This is the initial period when all we want to do is sleep with you. We've probably met you for five minutes but you have a great bust or ass, a pretty face and seem intelligent to talk to. Or not. Whatever. We will charm the pants off you. Hopefully. And that's the challenge for every man. It's a great high when you finally say yes.

2. Can You Leave Me Alone Stage: We've had the sex, done the poetry, cuddled and conversed our asses off. Now we need to be left alone to watch TV. Or play games on our Xboxes / PlayStations / Wii / Nintendo / Mobiles / iPads. Basically every gadget we have. We just need to zone out from you. Unless you're ready to have sex again.

3. Unshaved and Unbathed Stage: It's the weekend. Enough said. Either you're comfortable with that or you can move out.

4. Run Dude Run Stage: The families have met. The best friend likes us. The date for the wedding is almost set. And no man knows how the fuck he got from casual sex to commitment for a lifetime in such a short time. Even if he's been engaged for fifteen years. Now is the time to run. Before the bride goes shopping. Who am I kidding. She's been shopping for her wedding day since she was sixteen. Her parents have been saving gold jewellery for her since she was five. You're truly doomed if you don't stand up and speak now. Maybe even lie a little. Tell them you have herpes. That'll do the trick. All the best.

Lengtu was truly stuck. I wondered if I would get leave to go to his wedding. I needed to be with my cousin during his difficult time. But before I could ponder about his day of mourning, stage four arrived for me.

Radha called me in office on a regular hourly basis. Just to check if I was there near the landline, or I had gone off with some woman. I often thought that if I *did* want to go off with another woman, I would easily make it back in fifteen minutes. I didn't need longer than that. In my head, I had tricked Radha and was feeling very smug. 'Hello Radha, quickly speak, I'm getting into a meeting.' I put down my fifth cup of tea and *Mid-Day* crossword. There was no work really, but who wanted to speak to a woman while you're in office unless it's the hot programming chick who had been eyeing me.

'Don't make any plans for this weekend. We're going to Pune to meet my parents.'

What the...

'Radha we've discussed this. I don't have any money to commit more than I already have now,' I said, hoping she would remember the logic I had given for the last two years.

'Don't lie to me. I know you've got a big fat Diwali bonus. And if you don't commit now, then you're only using me. So we're meeting my parents and that's the end of the discussion.'

She hung up leaving me choking on my tea and pride. I was just using her in a way. But she was using me too. I thought that was what comprised relationships. Wasn't it? How did she get to know about my bonus? Then it hit me. My bank statements came home and she must have opened it to check how much I had. No wonder she would spend money on herself and leave just enough to pay the bills. Bloody sneaky woman.

I put down the phone just as I was called into a meeting. The day had not started well and it wasn't going to get any better. Tweedledee and Tweedledum were sitting on either side of the large conference table with their respective teams by them. The CEO, Nincompoop, was screaming at someone already. Apparently, the programming team had screwed up a sales integration and it was affecting everyone. I sat down slowly in a corner, hoping no one would notice me and I could leave early.

Suddenly it dawned on me. Mumbai had not been easy for me. I'd been stuck in the same job for the last three years. I'd been stuck with the same girlfriend for the last two years. And I was nowhere closer to my dream of a Lamborgini or Sunny Leone. I stayed quiet all through the meeting. Sometimes we all need to just go with the flow so we can get our cheques at the end of every month. Life isn't all about standing up and speaking out when you have rent to pay and a clingy girlfriend who sucks up all your resources.

With five minutes to go before the end of the meeting, Nincompoop looked at me and said, 'Obro will tell us the numbers on the Top 20 Countdown Show. Obro, where is your presentation?'

Now I'd had no clue I was to make a presentation. I didn't have anything prepared. I sat stunned as forty people turned to look at me. I couldn't even stutter. I only wanted to kill Nincompoop and then have a big black hole open up and swallow me.

I stood up and cleared my throat. Then I remembered how I had got out of so many situations in the last two years with Radha; surely I could figure out a way to do that now as well. 'I had a long presentation prepared but since we only have five minutes left, I can tell everyone the details in brief, if it's okay with you, sir?'

Nincompoop shrugged and said, 'Carry on.'

I started speaking, spouting some jargon I had memorized about all the shows. I tried to correlate them somehow with each other. I spoke and spoke until I ran out of breath and that's all Nincompoop wanted to hear because he was on the phone most of the time anyway. Then he raised his hand and said, 'That's enough Obro. You've made your point that you know nothing. Next time, be better prepared.'

He walked out of the room as the forty people there began to snigger at me. I felt completely humiliated.

A young marketing intern came up to me and said, 'You're Obrokranti Banerjee, aren't you?'

I looked away, too embarrassed to say anything. I looked down at my phone. There had been twenty missed calls from Radha while I was giving my speech. I was fed up. She probably wanted to figure out what I would wear to meet her parents.

'What you said actually made sense, Obro. The boss didn't hear it because he was on the phone with his girlfriend.'

Suddenly my ears caught on. 'What?" I asked. 'How did you know he has a girlfriend?'

She smiled with a twinkle in her eye. 'I may be new here, but I observe everything. I was a journalist earlier with *Stardust*. It was my job to overhear everything and dig out news about people.'

I marvelled at her. *Stardust* was an amazing magazine. It was far better than *Time* or *Newsweek*. It was the Holy Grail of Gossip. It was every man's secret read in the bathroom. She picked up her purse and said, 'He is quite an ass though. Not like you. You're so smart to think of all those correlations in such a short time.'

I gloated just a little. 'Well I have made a two-hundred slide deck.'

'Really? That's incredible.'

I smiled widely. The humiliation in the boardroom felt a little less depressing now. 'Would you like to share my dabba with me?' she asked, and I knew I was on a date!

Both of us went to the canteen and picked up the overused, ancient plastic plates that had probably been lent to this office after a catering company had used them at a hundred weddings.

'What's your name?' I asked her as she sat down opposite me.

'Anu.'

'That's a pretty name,' I said and flirted for the first time with another woman. I felt like quite the dude. I hadn't called Radha back and here I was having lunch with a pretty marketing intern called Anu.

Anu served me some of the fried fish she had brought and I fell in love with her at that instant. She had made fish and she had served me. I could get down on one knee and propose to her. I looked at her more carefully. She had decent-sized breasts. Not as great as Radha's, but shapely enough. She had long black hair and almond-shaped eyes, like Ma Durga. That's all I needed. A beautiful, benevolent woman who could be great in bed and cook fish for me.

We started chatting about how Nincompoop liked to humiliate everyone just to feel better about his own life. He was a cheap bastard who took the credit for everyone's work and hardly did anything on his own. He flirted with young women and cheated on his wife. Yet he was paid two crore a year as CEO. It was so unfair. The rest of us struggled like mad, worked our asses off and were much better workers than him, and yet got paid a pittance.

'Well the law of a corporate office is that the bigger the dumb ass, the fatter the pay cheque,' she said.

'Well that means I'll never get to buy a Ferrari then,' I bragged, but with sarcasm. She laughed out loud at my wit. I could see I had captured her heart.

I liked talking to Anu. She was smart and she understood me. I would take her under my wing and teach her the ropes. I would be her mentor. I would make her soar, under me. In more ways than one. My day-dreaming was cut short by a presence looming near the entrance of the canteen. Several people had turned to see what was there. I was still smiling and laughing when Anu looked over my shoulder in that direction as well. She looked at me and said, 'Obrokranti, do you know that girl?'

I knew it then. The hair at the back of my neck stood. I should have called her back. I had no business having lunch with another woman. I would live to regret this moment. It would come back to haunt me years later when my life was more settled. I turned slowly and saw Radha standing at the entrance of the canteen with the security guard who had escorted her inside. I got up, fumbling, while the entire canteen watched me.

'Radha, I...'

Anu moved away to the bathroom. The canteen people stopped in their tracks to look at me and those who had finished their lunch returned to their seats and happily watched the action.

Radha raised her hand and I stopped talking. She came closer to me. 'How could you?' she hissed. 'How could you have an affair with another woman?'

Affair? I'd just had lunch. I started explaining this when Radha's voice echoed in the canteen, 'I don't want to hear it! You betrayed me. You cheap bastard.'

I shook my head vigorously and said, 'Anu and I just met.'

'Ohhhhh. You're calling her *Anu*, is it? Are you defending her?'

I shook my head again. 'No.'

Anu had come out of the bathroom and was listening to all this.

Radha continued, 'I can't believe you would do this to me. You're a lying scumbag. I knew you would be a womanizer. How many women in this office have you slept with?'

'Radha, no one.'

Radha turned and said, 'You will have to answer to my entire family. Come home right now.'

See, at such points in a man's life, it's best to go with the flow. Do as the woman says, and not what your brain suggests. Stupidly I looked at my watch and said, 'It's only two o' clock. It'll be considered a half day if I leave. And boss might need me here.'

'Am I not important to you at all? What about my feelings? Don't you want to talk about this?'

I wiped my hands on a napkin, looking down at the food that was left uneaten. 'Can't we talk about it when I get home at night?'

Fuming, Radha turned and walked away. I thought that would be the end of the conversation but Anu came out from hiding and silently packed her dabba.

'Anu, I'm sorry Radha said all those things about you,' I said.

Anu looked me straight in my eye and said, 'It wasn't what Radha said that disappointed me Obrokranti. It was how you didn't defend me. You only thought about yourself.' She went back to her desk with a few other female colleagues surrounding her, all of them giving me dangerous murderous stares.

Great. Now I had two women who were angry with me and I had no idea why. Not only did I need to pacify two hormonal creatures and convince them I was not the bad guy in this entire situation, I was probably never having sex again.

25

I went home to find Radha sitting on the bed in a house that had obviously been struck by a hurricane. If not, there would be no reason to have all my clothes, books, and toiletries all over the floor.

'What the hell happened here?' I asked.

'You. You happened here.'

I put down my backpack and looked around for somewhere to sit. I hoped she would get me a cup of tea. But I was sure she would do something drastic if I asked.

'Why did you do this, Radha? There is a simple explanation to what happened today.'

Radha took a pillow and threw it at me. 'I know. You're sleeping with that whore.'

'Are you mad? I was having lunch with her. She's an intern.' How had she made me do this? Just the other day I was planning to manipulate her into breaking up with me, and here I was, defending myself to her. The truth was, Radha was perfectly capable of going to my boss, and accusing me of sleeping with an intern. Then he would fire me and I wouldn't have a job. Now that's a really depressing state to be in.

'You're screwing your boss' wife and now an intern? What is it, Obro? Am I not enough for you?'

'No, you are, Radha,' I said. This was not the line of questioning I wanted to follow. This is the reason why men can't break up decently with women. They take everything we say and convolute it horribly; it's just easier for us not to call them ever again and hope they get the hint that we're not interested in the relationship anymore.

'Do you know how much I've given to you? My life has been devoted to looking after you.'

Women exaggerate everything. I was standing there wondering how two years could constitute an entire life. And what had she done for me really? I had brought her to my place. I paid the rent. I bought the groceries with my money. I paid all the bills and I managed her shopping as well. What the hell was she doing? How was she contributing to me monetarily?

So the only thing that came out of my mouth was, 'Huh?'

'Don't look so dumb, Obro. I've made sure you've had a clean house, starched clothes, good food and managed your social life so you don't go off the deep end with drugs and alcohol. I've looked after your emotional and sexual needs, and all you can say is huh?'

I honestly didn't get it. How was all that equivalent to the money I'd spent on her? I also gave her sex. She wasn't just lying there; she also had fun. I presume. And I gave her a house to clean and my clothes to starch. If I hadn't given those to her, she would not be able to give anything back to me.

'I don't think we understand each other anymore,' Radha said as she paced the floor.

She was right. We didn't. 'You just don't think of me as a priority,' she continued.

Priority? She had always been a priority. If she hadn't been there, my career would have soared. But I always came home to her. I didn't network with the people in office. I could have impressed so many of them by now if I didn't have to come home to her every night to pander to her needs.

'You are so immature. You need to grow up and accept reality.'

What reality? How was I immature? I was the one who was working my ass off to survive in this city.

'Take responsibility for a girlfriend. Of your life. What are you doing with your career? Is this what you want to do for the rest of your life? Don't you have any ambition to do something more?'

'I'm trying,' the only words that squeaked out of me seemed hollow even to me.

'You have issues. You need to get therapy,' Radha said. And all I could do now was nod. 'No woman will want to be with you if you can't stand up for her. Love is not an easy thing. You can't just say the words and remain the way you are. You need to make an effort. Take responsibility. If you don't change your attitude now, you'll never get anywhere in life.'

I wondered what attitude she was talking about. Had I been so awful? Suddenly I knew I didn't want to be alone. Maybe Radha was the only one who would tolerate me for so long. Maybe I wasn't such a success in my career. I needed to learn and become better. Was what she was saying correct? Did I need to try and become better as a partner?

Suddenly I wanted to prove that I could make this work.

That I wasn't a loser in her eyes. Maybe it was all *my* fault. I was the one who was breaking Radha's heart. I was the one who had gone drinking on the eve of her birthday. I was the one who broke the fast I promised to keep on karva chauth. I was the one who didn't call her when she wanted me to.

I realized that she was just insecure about me. I was the one who was making her insecure. A woman is clingy when she relies on you for everything. It's probably because she doesn't have a social life outside of you. She didn't have any friends. I was the one she leaned on. I suddenly realized that her family rarely called her. Maybe she was here with me to get away from them.

I needed to love her even more. I was taking her for granted. I decided that I would take charge of this relationship and show her that I could be a better man.

Little did I realize that her reverse psychology tactics had worked with me. Instead of breaking up and getting my freedom, I had been pulled even more into the relationship with my clingy girlfriend.

26

I was extra sweet to Radha over the following few weeks. She decided to postpone the meeting with her parents until she had decided that I was the right one for her. I was obsessed with proving that I was. I even told Menon to tell Anu I could no longer talk to her. I thought it was the decent thing to do. Either I could be faithful to my girlfriend and never talk to another woman again, or I could go up to Anu and have a long dialogue with her about why I couldn't talk to her. I had to pick. It had to be Menon. It backfired big time. I overheard the girls in Anu's group calling me a 'rude scumbag'. I had no idea why. Maybe something was lost in translation.

'What did you say to Anu?' I asked him, noticing that she was glaring at me in a conference meeting. I was sitting next to Menon, and Tweedledee and Tweedledum were talking some nonsense about a new music band and their marketing tactics.

'I told her that you weren't interested in talking to her anymore.'

Menon was an ass. I decided then and there that there was no point in asking him to do anything for you because he would botch it up. 'That's not what I told you. I told you to tell her that I was a committed man and I didn't want to hurt my girlfriend so I could not be interested in anything but her even if I really want to be Anu's friend.'

'Ya, that's what I meant,' Menon said as he played a game on his new iPhone. I looked at it and wondered how such an idiot could afford an iPhone when all I had was a junk piece from the time when they hadn't even coined the phrase 'smart phone'.

Just then Radha called again and I answered again. I whispered into the receiver so my bosses wouldn't hear, 'Hi. I'm in a meeting. Can I call you back?'

She replied, 'Keep it on for a minute so I can hear if you really are in a meeting.'

And so I did. I turned the speaker slightly to the rest of the room and Radha could hear Tweedledee asking Anu what she thought about the music band. Anu replied.

I whispered into the receiver again, 'See, I'm in a meeting. Now can I hang up?'

'I don't understand why you still don't get me,' Radha replied.

'What?' I whispered back, confused.

'That slut is in a room with you and you expect me to be okay with it?'

'But she's not even sitting near me, and I don't talk to her anymore.'

'Even then. You just don't consider my feelings at all.' And then Radha did what all women tend to do to get their way. She began to cry.

Holy crap.

'Radha, please don't cry. What do you want me to do?'

'You should know me by now to know what you have do to make me feel better.'

'Sex? Now?'

'Not sex, you idiot. You have to leave the room. I can't stand you being there with that woman.'

I looked around and saw Tweedledee staring at me. I could either hang up and keep my job, or I could console my clingy girlfriend and keep my relationship. I whispered, 'Okay.' I kept my phone by my side and walked up to Tweedledee and whispered to him so Radha wouldn't hear, 'It's Swaty ma'am.'

Tweedledee nodded and gestured for me to take it outside. The lies I had to weave to keep my relationship intact were pure genius even to me. I felt like Jason Bourne. Leading a double life.

'I've come out now, please can you stop crying?' And magically, within moments, Radha stopped as if I had turned off the tears switch.

'I'm so glad, Obro. Now I know you love me. You have proved it. For now.'

Women are always testing us. The games never stop. They're never happy. They will always ask us questions like, 'How much do you love me?' What shit is that? How can I measure or prove how much I love you? If you don't believe me, take a hike woman. They'll test us with various tricks, like point a girl out and ask, 'Is she prettier than me?'

Most men don't know what to say, but I do: 'Of course not, honey. You're far prettier.' Then they ask, 'Is she thinner than me?' You're stuck then, because if you say yes, she will starve herself into such a bad mood, that she will eventually bite your head off. And if you say no, she will turn around and answer, 'Of course she is, you liar. So obviously you're just saying things to please me and actually you do think she's prettier than me.' Instead of realizing that we're saying things to *please them*, they turn around and sulk because they've pointed out a woman to us who we wouldn't have noticed anyway.

You can't win with women and bosses. No matter what you do, you're doing it wrong. Plus, you're constantly compared to someone better than you. You're never taller than so and so, or smarter, or wear sharper clothes or have a better body or make as much money. The man in a woman's life will always come up short. In more ways than one.

But hello, have you ever compared us to the bad guys out there? The slackers who do no work at all in offices or relationships? Why blame us? Look at how much you get instead of how much you don't. There are men out there who are bloody awful. And it's because they think they're God's gift to women, and it's the women who make them think so. Starting from their mothers, right down to their girlfriends, wives, mothers-in-law who think the *daamaad* can do no wrong, to their female colleagues who praise them no matter what.

So when you find a great man, I would recommend you leave him alone and not question every little thing about him. Stop with the rants like, 'You went out drinking again!' 'You didn't talk nicely to my best friend.' 'You didn't take Tommy for a walk this morning.' What the hell! Why? We are helpless creatures. Just because God made us stronger doesn't mean we will use that force against you. Don't talk about us to your other women friends unless you have something nice to say. When men get together, we don't talk about what women say to us. In fact, we respect them by ignoring them. We talk about sports, work and chutiyas in office.

Men should have rights too. We should be allowed to have as much freedom as women do. It seems to be okay to go shopping with a man's money and not contribute to the house at all. But if a man asks a woman to spend money at home or on him, then she takes a stand saying, 'This is not the way I was brought up. This is not what society demands of us.'

Women have freedom to wear what they want at all times and never have a man say anything to them. I say go for it. But then let us also roam in our underwear at home and scratch our balls when we want without women commenting or undermining us constantly.

Women make so many demands on men. Be strong, be courageous, be ambitious, be sensitive, caring, gentle, sexy, smart, great with your friends, humble to your parents, creative, rich. It goes on and on. And when we make a single demand, like make a cup of tea, suddenly their feminist side rears its ugly head. 'What do you think I am? A maid?'

I honestly want to also reply, 'What do you think I am? An ATM?'

Women are allowed to cry. Men are called sissies if they do. Women are allowed to make demands. Men are considered aggressive if they do. Women are allowed to play games in their relationships. Men are considered slimy if they do. The tilt towards women is increasing so much that today's man is at a loss as to how to tackle women. There are hundreds and thousands of articles on what women want and how to please them. But even if we follow all of them, women will come up with new desires and ways to be unhappy. Even though a woman knows what a man wants, she seldom gives in. She thinks it's below her dignity to give a blow job. Seriously then, get us a cup of tea!

Why do all women see men as potential to be moulded? Are we made of clay? Wasn't our mother a woman who brought us up correctly in any case? Don't we have a personality that you fell in love with? Then what is this great urge to 'polish the edges'. If we're soft and sensitive, they want to make us strong and macho. If we're strong and macho, they want us to be more humble and sweet. If we're comfortable with our jobs, they want us to be more ambitious. If we're driven, they want us to slow down and think about family more. If we're materialistic, they want us to be more spiritual. If we're leaning towards God and religion, they want us to see reality and live it up.

Women are unhappy creatures at heart. Men are their projects. And finally when we become the vision they wanted, they get bored of us and say, 'You're not the man I fell in love with. You've changed.' Well of course, we have. For you. So that you are happy in life and can leave us alone in peace. But they've moved on to another project by then, hoping to change some other man.

Women use their hearts to think. Their logic is a kind that only the female species understands. And there will be a bunch of women who will fill your girlfriend's head with new ideas and she'll come back and say the most absurd things to you. 'Why don't we ever go on a world tour? So-and-so is doing it.' Or, 'You never buy me anything nice. So-and-so's husband bought her the latest bag from Prada.' Or they will say, 'How come you never come to meet my friends?

Puja's husband always comes when we go out.' Truly, beware when your woman has a girls' night out or a brunch with her friends. She will either come back and want to change her wardrobe, change the house, or change you. And all three will be disaster for your pocket.

There is no introspection at this point. They never think that we have jointly decided to save our money for a house in the future. That her girl friend has enough things to fill an entire chawl, or that Puja's husband is probably a wuss without a life or male friends, and if you did land up to meet her friends all the time your girlfriend would probably think that you're a loser who always tags along with her. There's no winning for men.

But women are wondrous creatures to be explored. They have brains that can make men fall in love, laugh and be better human beings. They have breasts that are soft and luscious that men can sink into. They have strength and power that can move nations into action. They have sweetness that holds two families together. They are not the weaker gender to me. I can be under them anytime they choose. In fact, men would love to sit at home and let the woman go and work. I would gladly report to a female boss who can help me with my career, than a man who doesn't know how to balance his colleagues or his mistress. I would love for role reversal, role formation, role removal in this society as long as women would be happy.

And that was why I decided to do as much as I could to give this to Radha. I had chosen her. I would make sure she knew how much she meant to me.

27

One night I was sitting in Tweedledee's car waiting for him while he met his mistress. His wife and I had become quite close. I'm sure she suspected that her husband was having an affair, but since he gave her a nice house, a beautiful car and a lovely foreign vacation twice a year, she probably didn't care. She soon stopped calling often, and I got this opportunity to work on several things while I sat in the car with the AC on as my boss had a rollicking time with his girlfriend.

I downloaded many TV shows and watched them on my laptop. I went through the day's emails and replied to them. I even had a chance to work on some presentations and forwarded them to both Tweedledee and Tweedledum and BCC-ed Nincompoop. Let him also realize that I could do some work in this company after he'd humiliated me.

I would also call Radha and tell her what I was doing all the time so she had no need to complain. Radha realized that my boss was using me and felt bad that I had to go through it. She threatened to tell the wife one day but I explained to her how I needed this job. Until I found something else, I couldn't move. Radha understood, and believed I wasn't cheating on her, but she was upset that I had to come home late several times a month.

It was the first week of December and everyone was rushing around for year-end programming and marketing. What would the channel look like during the holidays? Who was taking leave? Who was getting a bonus? There was plenty of buzz in the office. Out of the blue, the CEO's secretary called to tell me that I had a meeting with him at four in the evening. Everyone around me wondered why the CEO wanted to meet me. I was shitting bricks. Maybe he'd heard I called him Nincompoop and decided to fire me. Or he'd heard I was roaming around with Tweedledee and surfing sites I wasn't allowed to and was firing me. Or maybe he realized that I was a Bengali who was too cultural for this stupid place and wanted to fire me. Anyway, it didn't look good for me at all.

At three o' clock I went to pee. I drank water and had a cup of coffee. I wanted to be hydrated and alert for my meeting. At three-thirty, I went to pee again. I had a nervous system that affected my bladder. At three forty-five, Radha called and I told her I was going in to see the CEO and I might be fired. All she could say was, 'Oh. Good luck.' What the hell did that mean? Good luck on getting fired or not? Bloody woman.

At four on the dot, I was set. I sprayed on my deo and followed the secretary to the CEO's office.

'Come in, Obro,' the CEO said as he swirled back in his chair towards his laptop and shut it slowly. I sat on the chair opposite him and folded my hands. He started to speak to me, but before he could say anything I burst out, 'Sir, I'm so sorry for anything you might have heard. I'm a dedicated worker. Please don't fire me.'

The CEO looked puzzled and then started laughing. The

Nincompoop was making fun of me before he let me go. I stood up in indignation. I would not stand for this.

'Sit down,' the CEO said more sternly, and I sat back quiet as a mouse.

'I'm not going to fire you. In fact I called you here to talk about your Feluda concept.'

Uh...

'You wrote an article on it. Don't you remember? It came as an email to me.'

I remembered. I had been reading one of the Feluda books, the super sleuth character that was invented by the mastermind Bengali, Satyajit Ray. The iconic private eye is well known amongst Bengalis, and every Bengali boy has read the Feluda stories or watched the films. I remembered that I had been sitting in Tweedledee's car one evening and had written out why Feluda should be brought to life for the youth of today. I had made the character of Feluda younger, a teenage super sleuth, a modern day Sherlock Holmes. I had written out the different characters, story, plot lines and climax that the show could have. But I didn't remember sending it to anyone.

'It is an extremely interesting concept. Tell me more about it,' Nincompoop said as he looked at me earnestly.

I started rambling at first, but then I became more confident about my idea. I had read so much of Feluda that I was well equipped to speak about it. I could see Nincompoop get into my story and the more I spoke the more he was intrigued. After almost twenty minutes, I stopped and took a deep breath. Either he thought I was a complete blabbering idiot or he thought I was a complete genius. I could not tell which. But I reached for the glass of water in front of me and took a large gulp.

'That's a very interesting idea, Obro. I think you should lead the team in getting it made.'

What the...

My jaw dropped to the floor.

'Excuse me sir?'

'I think we need to make a program that the youth can identify with. It can be fiction but with the modern-day elements that everyone is talking about. Teenagers nowadays are veering towards mystery and romance. If you can bring out both in this series that would be great.'

'But sir, I'm a marketing guy.'

'Great. So you write this out as a fifty-two episode show with the programming team. I'll tell them in the next meeting, and then you can work on it with marketing as well.'

This would mean so much work. I didn't want to give so much of myself. It would mean late nights and working on weekends. Radha would kill me.

'I'm honoured, sir, but...' I didn't know how to say the money I was getting wouldn't be worth the effort.

Nincompoop looked at me sternly. 'This is an opportunity of a lifetime, Obrokranti. To lead a team and show us how capable you are. You will get promoted after this to marketing manager. Don't let me down now.'

With that, he turned around and went back to the game of solitaire on his laptop.

All my colleagues were surprised I hadn't been fired. Bloody fools. I would show them I could become manager and then they would all have to report to me. All I needed to do was take Radha's permission to let me work. Because if she didn't, it might mean the death of my romantic life.

Five Ways to Get Out of Work

1. Delicate matters. It's easy to get a day off from work for personal reasons: diarrhoea, urinary tract infection, brain haemorrhage, tooth extraction, dog died, wife having a baby, car broke down, lice attack via your child. What you don't want to say is that you have a puja at home, a wedding to attend, are going with your girlfriend to a gynaecologist, moving house, no water in your house so you can't take a shower, or someone died. If your boss finds out you're lying, you can get fired.

2. Seniority superiority. Say you're already helping out on different projects in the office. Let your boss know that you're working on a project given by another boss, ideally his senior, and you will have to stop that and he might just get angry. Also, ask if he could speak to his senior to let you off his service. Your boss won't want to do that because he's probably shit-scared of his senior, in the process getting you out of this project for now.

3. Travel unravel. If you need to travel a lot and you really want to get out if it, you can cite air sickness, car sickness or any form of motion sickness that stops you from leaving the city too often. You can insist on working harder in office and making up for it. In addition, point to another person in the team who prefers flying anyway. Most bosses don't care who does the job as long as the job is done and it's not them doing it.

4. IT raid. Tell your boss that there are IT raids happening in the city and you've heard that his house is going to be targeted that day. He will probably rush back home giving you a day off.

5. Curious cat. If your boss calls and you're not in office, say you were on your way when you saw your boss' wife / girlfriend with another man at a coffee shop and they were getting cosy. You stayed to see what was really going on and you got late. Your boss will have too many things on his mind to bother if you come to work or not.

28

'You mean to tell me you're going to do MORE work for this place and they're not going to give you a raise? And it will keep you away in the evenings? I won't have it!' Radha shouted at me, throwing a few cushions while she was at it. I really don't know why women do that. When they're mad they throw things. The more violent the nature, the more breakable the item. If you're mad at someone, just hit them, like we men do. Why go with the intention of hitting something and completely miss since you don't know how to aim. That's where the term 'he throws like a girl' comes from. Also, what's up with all these cushions? Do we really need five hundred at home?

'Radha, if I prove to them that I'm capable, I get promoted. And all promotions mean more salary. But it's just a question of time. Unless I put in the effort, I won't be able to earn the money. Now please get me some dinner, I need to work out the details of this show.'

'Shut up! What about me? What will I do in the evenings while you're away? I thought you going on drives with your boss was bad enough, but now you have to work on top of it? When am I going to be a priority for you, Obro? I'm always the last person on your list.'

'I'm not working this hard for myself. I'm working hard for us. So that we have a future,' I said, partially believing it, and partially because I'd heard it was the best thing to say to a woman so she would lay off the guilt trip about not making her a priority.

'I'll see it to believe it,' she mumbled and left me alone to go heat up dinner.

That night she tried to have sex with me but I wasn't in the mood. This was the first time in my life that I was just too tired or too preoccupied to make love to her. I couldn't believe it. I never thought this day would come. I had the libido of a dog on a hot summer night. I felt terrible that I couldn't perform. And Radha didn't really care. She just turned over and went to sleep. But this was a huge deal for me. How could I not perform? Was this what people meant when they said the greater the power, the lesser the libido?

It was a known fact that as men grew in their company, they had less and less time for their spouses. Men work hard for their families and take on extra responsibility in their workplaces to keep their women and children happy. Unfortunately, though the bank balance may rise, the happiness quotient seems to diminish. Women are unsatisfied with men working late and not giving them enough sex. I can totally relate to this. If Radha worked all the time and didn't give me sex every night, I would be very upset as well.

Anyway, I went back to work and soon fell asleep on the couch. I would make it up to her twice tomorrow!

The next few weeks saw me in the office till late, working on the presentation with both departments and speaking to idiots who didn't get Feluda at all.

'Why don't we make him a Punjabi?' said TJ, who probably hadn't read a book since the Noddy series in kindergarten.

'We can have him fall in love with a really hot babe and they can do an item number in every episode,' suggested Abhijeet, who had a glad eye for every woman in the office and had several posters of Katrina Kaif in his cubicle.

With great responsibility must come great patience. Instead of moving on with the story, episodes, look, marketing, etc., we would get stuck on small details and argue about them for hours. After which, we all needed a coffee break, or if it was past sunset, we all went to the nearest quarter joint to have a few drinks and deliberate on the topic once again.

In three weeks, I had to make a presentation to the bosses on what we had planned, and they would then take a call on whether to go ahead with it or not. This was an important step on my path to success, and it was taking me forever to conceptualize the entire thing while keeping a budget in mind. I knew that if it became expensive to shoot, no one would want to do it, and then the blame for the idea being a flop would lie on my head.

One evening I was sitting quietly in front of the laptop when Radha came up to me. She had been awfully sweet to me. She had called me only twice an hour in office and if I didn't pick up, I could send her a mail on the new phone she had bought with my money. That way I could let her know what was going on if I was in a meeting instead of speaking to her.

'I have something to tell you,' she said.

I looked up briefly and asked, 'What?'

'My period is late. I might be pregnant.'

I looked at her in utter dismay. I had been very careful. I had been so careful that I had actually abstained from sex for many days. 'That's not possible.'

She sighed and sat down, 'We may be having a child in the new year.'

Fuck!

I couldn't believe this was happening to me. On the brink of failure, completely broke, unmarried, and now I would be a father to an illegitimate child? I could only drink myself to death.

'Are you sure?'

She nodded and smiled, 'Aren't you happy?'

No matter what relationship a man is in, when a woman tells him she's having her baby, there will be a moment of utter shock and complete silence. He will reflect in that moment how his days of drinking have gone for a toss and sleepless nights of nappy changes will begin; he will think of how he can't afford it and whether he will make a good father at all. All these things will happen for a second before he responds with exactly what the girl wants to hear, 'If you're happy, I'm happy.'

But if the man is not married and his girlfriend tells him she's pregnant, he will have a sudden fear as if he's in a jungle on a cold winter night and he hears a rustle amidst the trees behind him and he's just too afraid to turn around and check if it's a bear. Actually, that situation might still be easier than the one he is facing with his girlfriend. He wouldn't know whether to scream at her for not being careful enough because God knows it's also a woman's fault for getting pregnant. If in the heat of the moment she has said, 'Leave it off,' then it's her responsibility to take the necessary precautions the morning after. A man presumes she's done what is needed. Not trick him into having a child. A man cannot control his sperm and his desires. He's not the evolved species here!

'Raaaddhhhhaaaaa...' I began as a stutter. I honestly had no words.

'Where do you think we should have the nursery? I've gone online and picked out a crib. I think we may need to move. This place is way too small.'

I grabbed hold of her shoulders and said the most obvious thing that came to mind at the moment, 'Radha, we're not married yet.' What I really wanted to say was this was a disaster. My life was over. I didn't know what to tell my mother. What would my family think of me? Her family may kill me even before I could tell my family. This was a complete disaster. Yes that word kept coming back in my head.

'I know. That's why we need to get married soon. I'll make all the arrangements. It can be a small wedding. Just a mehndi, a sangeet and a wedding and reception. We'll organize it in a banquet hall. You don't worry about it. You just need to help me with the preparations whenever I call you.'

Fuckity fuck! Now I had to help her with a wedding for a baby I didn't want! My life was indeed over. A month ago, I was planning to break up with her, and now I was planning a life with her. And what about my presentation? My career? My great idea that would catapult me into fame and money? That would have to take a back seat for this woman who had planted herself in my life.

The entire evening went in going online and checking out baby names, baby clothes, baby furniture and wedding outfits. Several hours of precious time and several gigabytes of downloadable internet that I was paying for went in seeing the doom of my life.

29

The next week went in a haze with Radha calling me every five minutes to discuss if we should go with a red and gold theme for the Sangeet. She even told me she had met a designer downstairs who quickly became her friend and advised her on how to cover up her belly for the wedding. Please. She had already put on weight from sitting at home and eating junk food. She was already fat. Now she had an excuse for it.

Radha's mother had also been informed about the wedding and the entire family was now looking forward to meeting me. I had warned Radha that if any member of her family came to the house, I would walk out and never talk to her again. I needed to finish my presentation or there would be hell to pay. So she informed her mother that she was planning the wedding, but they would have to wait a few weeks before visiting us.

'I'm so excited that we're getting married and having a child. It's like we've been blessed twice over,' she gushed. I felt fucked twice over.

'Radha, I don't want to get married right now,' I said for the enth time.

'Well we can't bring a baby into this world and not be

married, so just deal with it,' she said. 'Do you want to have a temple wedding or a mandap in the lawns outside. I think if we have a temple wedding in the morning it would be quite lovely. I can wear a sari.' She continued for another half an hour while I tried to correct my presentation on Feluda and not pay any attention to her.

Men hate weddings. The only reason they attend weddings is for the open bar. And the drinks are probably in an uncle's Honda City which makes it even better – they don't even have to step inside the wedding area. The other reason is to ogle at women who will be all decked up wearing oodles of make-up and very little else to show off their slender midriff. An image we can carry back with us later and hump our wives with that thought. That's why everyone gets laid at weddings.

But no man really enjoys his own wedding. It's a day to mourn. And everyone around him seems happy and cheerful just to cheer him up. An entire family dances on the road to his grave. Just to keep him in good spirits. The bride however is dazzled with all the gold, clothes and presents she receives. She thinks that's love. But it's really not. If you tell her that love happens even if you don't get married, she'll look at you as if you're a creature from another planet that needs to die so the rumour dies with you.

But all women dream about their wedding. What they'll wear, who will be there and other such rubbish. And because they've been doing it for such a long time, they become control freaks when it comes to their wedding. They want everything perfect, otherwise their grand illusion comes crashing down. They feel that they've not accomplished even this little bit of an event, how will they manage a marriage.

Men on the other hand know they can handle anything. Except a sobbing bride who can't find her gold shoes.

I called up Lengtu one night when I was feeling terribly depressed. We spoke about everything but our relationship troubles and laughed about the idiots in our life who couldn't handle anything.

'Lengtu,' I said finally, 'Radha's planning a wedding.'

'Oh,' he said. 'When?'

'For next month.'

'Don't you want to tell everyone?'

'I'm still hoping to get out it.'

'Aaah.'

Pause.

'How should I get out of it?'

'Have you tried the *kundli*?'

'Ya. Apparently it matches.'

'Aah.'

Pause.

See this is the reason why men don't really chat about personal problems. It's far easier to chat about bosses, bikes, chicks and cricket. It's uncomplicated.

'Well, all the best, bro,' he said and called his sister Nandini to the phone. I heard him mutter, 'Pantha is in deep shit. Talk to him.'

So when I started chatting with Nandini I could actually confess my problem, 'Radha is pregnant.'

Immediately Nandini caught on to Radha's game. 'Are you sure?' she asked.

'What do you mean? She told me!'

'She's not tricking you?'

'I don't know,' I said, suddenly unsure if all this drama of a baby and a wedding was just to get attention from me.

Exactly what a clingy girlfriend would do. But how could I be sure it was not real? Before it was too late.

'Listen, don't tell anyone right now. You take her for a blood test to confirm the pregnancy. Be there when the doctor gives back the results. Don't rely on those pregnancy tests. They're all useless.'

As I listened to her advice, my mind was in a whirl. If Radha was lying to me, she must be deeply insecure and truly a psycho. When a woman goes to such great lengths to keep you in the relationship, it can only mean one thing. She has no one else in her life. But men and women can't fulfil every role in their partner's life. I couldn't be there for Radha every minute of every day in any case. What would happen to my life? My dreams? My goals? And my sex with Sunny Leone? If Radha wasn't lying and I was going to be a father, she would make sure I was home every evening to look after the baby and stay awake all night long changing nappies, burping the baby and whatever other shit fathers did. My lifelong ambition of travelling the world (one which every Bengali has) would go for a toss. I would only be travelling to McDonald's. And I didn't even like the food there!

I had to take Nandini's advice. Over the weekend, I would take Radha to the doctor for a blood test to determine if she really was pregnant. She might not like the idea but then she had no choice in the matter.

Honestly, they say having or not having a baby is solely a woman's decision. But I don't think so. It wasn't simply the man's decision to have sex. It was also the woman's decision to not take precautions to prevent the pregnancy. So if it was both parties' fault, it should also be both parties' decision whether to have the child or not. And no matter what the woman says about raising the child on her own, she will always resent the man for not being there.

There's no winning for a man if the woman gets pregnant out of wedlock. He has two options: either he can run and never look back and have the woman resent him for the rest of her life. Or he can stay, help look after the baby and hear her crib about how he never has enough time for his family because he's working to look after the family. Either way you're screwed. Because with the first, the guilt will kill you. For The Rest Of Your Life. And with the latter, the nagging will slowly kill your ego and soul.

So no, dear woman. It's not just your choice to have the baby or not. We fell in love with you / your body. Love, sex and romance are roughly the same thing. And it should be a joint decision if we want to raise a child. It may be your body. But it is our life. Men want to stay in the relationship. And not having a child doesn't mean we LOVE you any less. It only means we are not ready to love someone else right now. And no amount of tiny baby clothes, teddy bears and the glow on your face will change our mind. We might smile through it all and look happy on the outside, but inside we would rather postpone this decision till at least some of our dreams are fulfilled. Our dream, you see, was not to get married and raise great kids. It was to fall in love and make something of ourselves. It's about time that women help men realize their dreams instead of asking us to help them realize theirs.

In office, I continued to juggle presenting Feluda to the programming team and taking calls from Radha about the baby and the wedding. I almost had a heart attack from the stress. One day I was sitting in the canteen alone when Radha called for the fortieth time that morning. I pressed silent and immediately Radha sent me an email saying, 'You must be busy but can you tell me if you want a DJ at the sangeet or should we have everyone sing old songs?'

I honestly didn't care. Details about the wedding, baby and Feluda suddenly evaporated from my mind. I decided to go out and smoke. Just as I was walking outside, Menon passed by. I pointed to the balcony outside the canteen where we could light up. He nodded. He would join me.

We sat outside in complete silence for so long that I could actually clear all the thoughts in my head. Exactly what I needed. He finally cleared his throat and said, 'Great job with Felu, man. This is exactly what this channel needs.'

I nodded and said, 'Thanks.'

'You don't look happy. Gas?'

Men blame unhappiness on indigestion. This is a fact. They don't know any emotional, mental or physical state of pain other than diarrhoea.

'Probably,' I said. 'Also Radha may be pregnant and is planning a shotgun wedding.'

Menon looked at me with wide eyes and said, 'Dude, you're screwed!'

I nodded. Of course I was. 'My life is over unless a miracle happens.'

'Good luck, man,' Menon said as he stubbed out his cigarette and went inside. And that was that. Men didn't talk about their troubles. We just supported each other. And every man was in some kind of a mess. If one unloaded on another, you would have to share your troubles and then we'd all become women. Too complicated.

Just then a miracle occurred.

Radha called. I picked it up this time. She was sobbing. 'Radha, calm down. I can't understand you. Speak slowly.'

Radha spoke between sobs. 'I...lost...the...baby.'

30

Needless to say, I took another half-day and went rushing back home. The HR person in my office warned me that if I took off anymore, she would have to cut my salary for a full day. I had already taken ten sick leaves and ten casual leaves this year and about a dozen half-days. But I felt unexpectedly distraught. Suddenly I realized that maybe I had grown accustomed to the thought of being a father. Or maybe the idea had been slowly settling into my head before it was snatched away. I knew I needed to comfort Radha, but I wanted some comfort too. And no matter what men feel about having a child, they never want to lose one.

'It just happened an hour ago.' She sat on the sofa sobbing while I looked around wondering how I could console her.

'Shall we go to the doctor?'

She shook her head. 'I'll get over it.'

When women say they'll get over it, they won't.

'I just need some space,' she said as she walked into the bedroom.

And when they say they need space, they actually mean they need you to keep asking if they're doing okay. Because if she truly needed space, she wouldn't have asked me to come home. She would have dealt with this tragedy alone and spoken to me at the end of the day when I came back after completing all my work. We needed to be each other's comfort at this point. But men are bad in asking for comfort and the gender roles in society always say that men should be strong when handling loss. This is not true at all. We just have no platform to reveal our true feelings.

'Radha, come sit here, love. Tell me all about it,' I said. She sat next to me and sobbed into my shirt.

'Well a whole month passed and suddenly I got my period today.'

I nodded and then suddenly it hit me. Didn't it take a month for the menses to come anyway? So did she think she was pregnant even before the mandatory time slot was over? That didn't seem correct.

'When do you normally get your period?' No man ever wants to have this conversation. It's not really that fun for us. But when you have a woman sobbing on your shoulders and mixed feelings about a baby you may or may not have had, you can deal with it.

'On the twenty-sixth day. And I can feel it almost immediately by the twentieth day if I'm getting it. That's why when I couldn't feel it, I knew I was pregnant. And now I've lost the baby. Our baby, Obro. Aren't you sad?'

Now here's the thing. In such situations, you can't give logic to a woman. Especially a howling woman. And this I learnt the hard way. 'Radha,' I said pulling away, 'you were never pregnant. How can you lose a child if you weren't having one in the first place?' She had tricked me!

'How can you say that? We've lost a child today and you're being so mean to me.'

How was I being mean? I was being logical. She was the one who had stressed me out for the last few days. When I was in the middle of the most important project of my life. And dealing with the fact that I was going to be a father. Plus her lies about her family and the impending marriage! And instead of being apologetic about it, she was hoping for sympathy? Women! How is it all about them all the time? When will they ever apologize for their own nonsense?

'I'm not trying to be mean. I'm just trying to tell you that it never happened. So don't be so upset over something that wasn't there. It's ludicrous.'

'Are you calling me insane?'

Yes, I wanted to say. But didn't, obviously.

'I'm just telling you to move on.'

She looked at me and said, 'Maybe you're right. Maybe I should just concentrate on the wedding now.'

What the...

I shrugged and said casually, 'Maybe we shouldn't rush the wedding now. We can take it easy. There's no hurry. Plan correctly.'

'Are you backing out again? Just when I've lost a baby.'

'Radha, you haven't–'

'Stop it! I know I've lost the baby. Even if you don't believe it. In fact, I can't believe that you're so unsupportive. I thought you would be on my side.'

'I *am* on your side.' Which other side was there?

'So let's get through this tragedy together by thinking of happier thoughts like the wedding.'

My temper started boiling. Maybe Nandini was right. Radha had been tricking me all along just to get married. And because I was in the middle of so much work, to get some attention from me.

'Radha, I don't want to get married! This wedding is off,' I said holding my ground.

'What? How dare you? You know what. I don't care anymore. I'm sick of this. We're over. I need a break.'

'Are you breaking up with me?' Suddenly I felt relieved. I didn't want to make this relationship work anymore. I wanted to be free and happy. I didn't want to get married and have children. And I was definitely done with Radha in my life. I could already visualize having my apartment to myself again. Me taking carefree vacations to Kolkata and Delhi whenever I wanted. Me not being stuck to the phone all the time in fear of Radha calling.

God was pouring miracles down on me. I knew my luck had changed. It had to do with the new pokhraj ring I had started wearing. I rubbed it for more luck.

'Yes, I am breaking up with you. I don't want to see you anymore. Goodbye, Obrokranti Banerjee.'

And with that she did the most logical thing in the world. She walked into my bedroom and banged the door shut. I called out to her, 'Are you packing?'

She opened the door just to say, 'No!' and went back inside.

I hesitated for a brief moment before saying, 'But we're broken up. Won't you be leaving now?'

She emerged again. 'I can't believe I wasted so much of my time on you! You just don't get me. I can't believe I was so stupid to think this relationship would work,' she yelled, and banged the door shut again.

'Ya. Okay. But when are you going?' I wanted to make sure I could invite my friends over without her hovering around.

'You're an insensitive bastard!'

Still no answer to the question!

'Radha...?'

She opened the door again, came out with her hands on her hips as if to guard the door, and said, 'So you're just going to kick me out in the middle of the night?'

I looked around and saw that it was the middle of the day. Only four o'clock. She could easily hail a cab and go back to her parents' tonight.

'Don't be so mean, Obro. I'll go when I'm ready. I've made this my house. I have stuff here. I'm the one who made you who you are. Without me, you would not have all this. I'll go when I'm good and ready. And till then you can sleep on the sofa.'

She banged the door shut, only to open it again to rant at me, 'And don't think I'm getting your shirts washed and ironed anymore or giving you food or a dabba. You're all on your own now. You can look after yourself!'

I couldn't believe it. On the one hand she had broken up with me, and on the other, she was refusing to leave my apartment. I didn't know what to do.

My clingy girlfriend had now turned into my psychotic ex-girlfriend.

Games Women Play to Irritate Us

1. Many moods: Women have mood swings faster than the speed of light. One minute she will be lovey-dovey and into you, and the next, she wants to murder you. If you ask her if it's PMS (premenstrual syndrome is a week before her period starts where your girlfriend turns from the perfect

woman to a werewolf), she'll bite your head off. The only way you can handle this is to tell her you're there for her and then leave her alone. Or get her some flowers to cheer her up. Cheap and cheerful. Make sure she's not allergic. Or she'll bite your head off.

2. Mental agony: Abundant questions to understand where you stand in the relationship. Do you love me? Am I fat? Is she prettier? How many kids do you want to have? Shall we get a puppy? These are all tests to gauge if you truly love her and if you're ready for a commitment. Don't fall for them. Say yes to the first one and then go with the flow. If you can't be honest with her now, then you're going to be lying through the entire relationship including on your wedding day by saying you'll be faithful to her for the rest of your life and regret it as soon as the words tumble from your mouth.

3. Attention span: Women like getting men's attention. They will flirt with their eyes, dance seductively on the dance floor and even brush up against you to use every body part they have so that they get your attention. They will be flirty, witty, sharp, intelligent and charming. And once you have fallen for all of this, she will not care for you. The challenge for her is gone. Just the way once a man goes to bed with a woman, the charm has truly worn off. If he's still with a woman, it must mean he really loves her. The only way to handle this is by giving her attention in spurts. Keep texts short and always be the first to hang up. If she still acts hard-to-get, leave her and move on immediately instead of trying to fix it. Also if she isn't into you, there's no point in chasing her. She can call the cops and get you into deep shit.

4. Demanding diva: A house, a car, new clothes, meeting

her friends, weekend parties, the list goes on. And she says she's doing it all for you. A man needs space and time. Women just don't get it. They're clingy and need attention. And when you tell them this, they'll go to the corner and sulk. Drive men completely insane. The best way to deal with this is to send her off with her girl friends for a brunch. She'll be out of the house and you can have some alone-time. And in case there's a match on that you really want to watch, arrange a spa day for her. Getting your space isn't cheap.

5. Non-stop blabber: What are you thinking? The sentence that every man dreads. Women, we're not thinking of anything. Or we're thinking about other women, and we won't tell you because it will upset you and we seriously don't want to get into a fight. So stop asking us inane questions. And if we don't answer, stop filling the silence with chatter. Aarti did this. Garima went here. Diandra's husband left her. Idle gossip, opinions, planning for the future, ideas, dreams, criticizing others, comparing yourself and talking to us about it annoys us. Men do not want to be your best friend who you can share everything in your head with. They want to be a part of your life. Not share your entire life. Specifically minute-by-minute details of what's going on in your mind. We don't want to know. Nope. But if we tell women this they feel insulted. 'If I can't share my life with you, then what's the point of this relationship?' I'll tell you – sex. But we still love you and are faithful to only you. Just please keep the blabber to your friends. And don't tell us what your friends think of the blabber!

6. Flux capacitor: One minute she wants to spend her life with you and the next she's not so sure. One minute she's planning a wedding and then the next she needs a break. A

woman can go from being committed in this relationship to wanting to call it off and going back to being very in love with you within a day. The flaky flux capacitor makes it very difficult to gauge where you are in life. Women do this because they're still testing the waters. They don't know if they want to make that commitment to you or not. It's not really about you. It's about their heart. At this time, show all of your good and bad sides. Don't play the great guy role. Let her get to know you completely, and let her go if she doesn't like you for who you are.

7. Control freaks: The woman will slowly start picking at every aspect of you. It will start with your wardrobe: 'Are you really going to wear that?' And you'll ask, 'What do you want me to wear then?' And she'll start picking out your clothes. Then it'll be, 'Your teeth need cleaning.' And, 'Your snoring is terrible, go see an ENT specialist.' And soon it will be all about your diet, fitness and fashion. The three pillars that excite all women. She'll slowly start giving you healthy food, send you for a walk and throw away your favourite college shirt. Beware. They do this because they think it's their way of showing love. You must put down the rules of not changing from the beginning and even threaten to walk out if any change occurs. Good luck with that conversation. No man has succeeded.

8. Temporary amnesia: Women suffer from temporary amnesia. When they're upset they will forget all the great things you've done for them. And not only that they'll remember all the faults you have even though you've dealt with it together.

9. Sex games: To get what they want, they tell us they'll give us 'anything' we want in bed. And when we don't do as

they say, they deny us anything in bed. It's actually very frustrating. Because when we ask for all the things we want, they say – anything but that. And really then, isn't it just the ordinary that we've been getting all along? And if we finally put our foot down and refuse to give in to their demands, it may be when hell freezes over before we can get into a woman's pants again. One man on his sixtieth birthday finally turned to his wife and said, 'It's been fifteen years dear. Now can you let the argument go so we can have sex?' The wife turned and replied, 'Sure. But will you finally wear plaid pants like I asked you to?'

10. Clothes quotient: Women judge men by the clothes they wear. An old pair of jeans and a casual shirt says that you're a cool kind of guy. A formal shirt and trousers shows that you are a determined over-achiever. And designer wear shows that you're worthy of having any woman in the room. But none of that matters. Because ultimately all women will change your clothes and your dressing sense to what they like. What they want. And how they perceive their man to be. If they've seen Shah Rukh Khan wear pink shirts with faded jeans, rest assured she'll go off with your credit card and buy the outfit for you. Never mind if you're the laughing stock of the party later, at least your girlfriend has dressed you the way she likes. So be prepared to throw out your wardrobe and be made into a brand new man. Don't put your foot down. It's actually quite easy to look like a factory product since all women will follow the same trend that their friends do. Pretty soon you'll have no originality left until you become single again. And then a new woman will push you to wear clothes that she likes.

It's no joke that women will always have the upper hand.

That's why men need to stick together. Or we'll be a dying species!

Great insight: Adrian tells Rocky in *Rocky IV*, 'You can't win!' Rocky, the simpleton, thought she meant against Ivan Drago. You just can't win.

31

Even if the relationship status says 'broken up', it's really just 'complicated'. Because no man is ever truly free of his girlfriend till he moves to another country. Women will track you down and hound you for an explanation about why the relationship failed every minute of every day. And then they make you feel guilty that they broke up with you, when in fact you didn't have anything to do with the argument in the first place. That's why men would rather not pick up the phone or call their ex-girlfriends back. They would rather fade quietly away into the night and change their phone numbers if they can avoid explanations as to what went wrong and how they should patch up one last time.

I had thought things were bad when we were together, but they just got worse after we broke up. Not only did I not have my home back to myself, I had an extremely angry, supposedly ex-girlfriend who was still living there because she wanted to prove how much she had done for me. The calls stopped, and I was so relieved – but then the messaging started. She would text me several times a day saying random things like, 'I know you don't care but I have told the designer not to make our wedding clothes. I can't believe you can

move from "let's get married" to "let's break-up in a heartbeat".
As if my feelings don't count.'

I would reply, 'I never said "let's gets married", and thank
you for cancelling the wedding outfits.' Which was the truth.

And she would text back, 'I know you were just using
me. You really didn't care about me at all.'

And then several messages would go back and forth till I
would ultimately call for a conversation in which I would try
to defend myself and Radha would accuse me of new things
every hour. The harassment post break-up is worse than the
torture in a jail cell.

Sometimes Radha would call and sob on the phone, 'I
haven't eaten all day. Why did you do this to me?'

And I would step out of a meeting with the programming
and marketing departments about my vision of Feluda and
tell her in a calm manner, 'Radha, please go eat something.'

'Don't tell me what to do. You've lost the right to tell me
anything anymore.'

And I would want to tell her that she was doing this to
herself. If she didn't eat, she would be miserable. And she
was the one who had broken up with me. More than that, I
wanted to tell her that she was still living in my house, and if
she truly wanted to be free then she needed to leave.

Things were no better when I reached home. One day she
locked me out of the house saying I didn't deserve to enter. I
had to call the landlord and make him open the lock. He
warned me that this was the last time he was going to do it
because he didn't want to interfere in domestic affairs.

One day, Radha refused to speak to me the entire evening,
instead muttering to herself about how terrible I was and
what all her friends said about me. It was far more annoying

to not be able to listen to Arnab rant than to try and hear what Radha was saying in a barely audible voice. Because either she should just say what she wanted, or keep it to herself. No. The woman muttered all evening.

Another day I walked into the bathroom, picked up my toothbrush and noticed that it looked a little odd. Radha was watching me from outside. I suddenly saw her glance towards the toilet and then I realized that she had cleaned the toilet with my toothbrush. I immediately threw it away and took hers and brushed my teeth. She was so annoyed, but I didn't care. That was a dirty trick.

The thing that got to me though, was when Radha went through my laptop at night while I was sleeping and deleted the porn on it, which I hadn't had time to transfer to a hard disc. When I asked her a few days later what happened to it, she replied innocently, 'I don't know.' Playing innocent wasn't one of her strong points though, so when I hounded her, the reply I got was, 'I can't believe you care more about your porn collection than me.' Well of course I did. Now that we had broken up, porn was all I had.

Men are not good with break-ups. I asked Menon what I should do and he told me to date again. So logically, you have let go of one woman because you think she was psycho only to date another one because you didn't learn your lesson the first time. You know why we go on dating new women even though we know it will be the same pattern? For sex. And sometimes we may just hit upon the right girl who loves and appreciates us and looks after us the way we want, in and out of bed! Then we stupidly marry her and dig our own graves.

I joined a dating site and filled in my profile. I may have

exaggerated a few things like my height and my income. I got a few responses in my email inbox and was curious to see where it would go. I was looking forward to meeting new women and falling in love all over again.

Not to be.

Radha found my emails, tracked it back to the dating site, changed my preferences, and wrote back to the women who had responded. A phone call came to me while I was in office, and someone asked me to never get on any matrimonial site again or I would be reported to the cyber police. I was blocked from the site too.

There went my chances of finding anyone online. Jealousy fuels passion. Suspicion fuels obsession.

Radha began to use me in so many new ways that I never saw coming. One day I got an SMS alert from my bank saying that five grand had been withdrawn from my account. I immediately called them and said there had been some mistake. But they said that Radha had signed on it and it couldn't be reversed. I wondered what she had bought that had emptied out the amount I sent to my mother every month.

When I got home I saw that she had cut her hair into a bob cut and streaked it with some hideous yellow colour. 'Yikes! What have you done?'

She ran her fingers through her hair and said, 'I wanted a change. It's called a break-up makeover! I want to be someone new. I don't want to depend on you anymore. I'm independent and ready to meet new people.'

'With my money? That's just ridiculous. Well, you're most welcome to leave then. Go, be independent!' I said taking out a suitcase I owned so she could pack her things and get out of the house.

'I can't believe you're so insensitive. Instead of complimenting me on my new look and new attitude, it's all about you again. When will you grow up and act like a man? You make me sick.'

And yet not sick enough that she would leave. She took her plate of food and sat in front of the TV, hoarding the remote so she could watch a soap opera about a village where everyone wore make-up to sleep.

It didn't end there. One day Radha put a red top in with all my white shirts and underwear. Everything came out pink. It ruined my most expensive shirts and I felt like a girl wearing pink Rupa underwear. Since she had spent all my money, I couldn't even go and buy anything new for myself. But I let it go. She was hurting and I had to be supportive. Soon she would see the error of her ways, apologize, and hopefully leave.

But the next day I came home to find Radha had torn up all the photos of us and trashed everything. There was a fire in the middle of my Lilliputian drawing room. 'Radha, what the hell are you doing?' I said, running to the bathroom to get a bucket of water to douse the inferno.

'I needed to get rid of everything that reminded me of you. I couldn't torture myself being surrounded by things that were of us. A happy us. An us that is over.'

'So you make a bonfire? In the house?'

'Relax, it's all under control.'

But apparently it wasn't. The fire alarm went off and the fire trucks came and people surrounded our apartment and the landlord warned us that if we tried anything funny again I would get evicted. Of course Radha got all the sympathy from her female friends in the building who gave me dirty looks for not supporting her decision to get rid of things that were hurting her. Things that also included stuff that was important to me, like the tie I wore when I came first in tenth grade, and a photo of my family that I kept on my night dresser. I wondered how all my stuff hurt her. I dared not ask, though. And it seemed to have worked – for a few days, there was some kind of peace at home. Then, on a Wednesday afternoon, Menon came up to me while I was smoking in the balcony and said, 'Dude, your ex is here.'

'Fuck. In office? What is she doing here?' I asked throwing my cigarette away.

'Maybe she's come for a job,' Menon said. I thought I would die. If she got a job in the same place as me, she would stalk me day in and day out. This would be an utter nightmare.

I went inside and saw Radha sitting in Tweedledee's cabin. She spotted me through the glass windows and waved to me. I scowled back. After five minutes, she walked ut of Tweedledee's office and came up to me. 'Hi Obro. What a coincidence.'

Coincidence? When she had come to *my* office. Where she *knew* I would be. Women say the stupidest things at times. 'You better be careful with your boss,' she continued. 'He's quite angry with you. Good bye!'

With that, she left, heading home – to my house. My boss called me into his cabin. I knew I was getting fired.

'Obrokranti, you told your fiancée about me? About where we go, and what we do?' I shook my head, speechless. He thundered on, 'Now she's planning to blackmail me. I'm telling you – if I'm going down, I'm taking you with me.'

Anything with the word 'down' should never be said by a man. I was going to tell Tweedledee this, but decided to focus on the matter at hand instead. I realized it would be best to confess everything to him. 'Sir, she's my ex-fiancée. And she's just taking revenge. I'm sure you've been in my place, sir. Trust me, I haven't told her where we go or who you meet. I've just told her that I'm with you.'

Tweedledee considered this and asked, 'So she doesn't know anyone's names?' I shook my head. 'Where they live?' I shook my head again. 'Or how much I pay my mistress?'

'You pay your mistress? Why, sir? Doesn't that defeat the purpose of free sex when you're in love?'

'Shut up. And get out.'

Thankfully I hadn't lost my job. Everything else could be managed. I went home and blew up at Radha, who could only sob and say how sorry she was that she'd said she needed a break, and that she wanted to get back together. She'd made a mistake, she said; she couldn't live without me.

And before I knew what was happening, we were somehow back together.

All I could do was wonder, with an ice pack on my head, how my miracle had turned into such a disaster.

32

The new year came. We returned to office on Thursday, after a day of rest, and I plunged into work. I was supposed to make my presentation on Feluda to Nincompoop the following Monday. With my romantic life being in such a mess, I was happy I had this at least. The program would be approved, I would be a hero, and given a huge promotion, I thought joyfully. But on Friday, my life was in shambles again.

Nincompoop hired someone to handle my project – and I would have to report to him. Nincompoop felt I was too junior to manage such a large project, so a new manager, Krishna Karikurve, had been recruited. He would be the go-between me and Tweedledee and Tweedledum. I was super angry that all my hard work would have to be shared with this idiot. And he would take all the credit when it became a hit. He was also the one who would get the money that would have been given to me if I had been made project manager. Now I didn't see a raise or a promotion anywhere and I had been slogging my ass off for over a month, despite my relationship issues!

I wanted to raise hell, but I knew I had to do as Nincompoop said, otherwise all my work would be in vain, and not only would they stop Feluda, but they would also fire me. Kurkure, as I liked to call him, because he was as twisted as the snack and added spice to everything he said, soon became my nemesis.

Krishna Karikurve was US-returned. By that I mean he had been in the United States for a marketing program for all of three months. He had an American accent, blond streaks and wanted to be called Kris. None of us complied, and the name I gave him stuck. Every time we yelled from one corner of the office to another, 'Hey Kurkure,' he would respond with the dude attitude: 'Call me Kris!'

I had to sit with this moron and explain my entire idea and presentation to him so he could present it to the board and take all the credit. I was given a week. More delays in my life. So I did so grudgingly.

'So this Feluda guy, is he like fuckin' gay?' Kris asked me. I gave him a murderous look.

'Why would you say that?'

'I don't know. He's Bengali, in a skewed relationship, and is a meek man. Kinda sounds homo, if you ask me.'

'Feluda was a character made by the great Satyajit Ray. If you saw *Sonar Kella* you would never even say that. Feluda is a mastermind. He's the young Indian Sherlock Holmes. But better because he has a wry sense of humour and can outsmart any Indian cop,' I said defensively. Not that I had anything against homosexuals, it was just that it wasn't the case here.

'So it's like the *Dhoom* series?'

I hit my head, 'No it's nothing like Bollywood or Yash Raj or the TV shows you've seen before. That's what makes this concept so exciting and new. The youth need a new icon to connect with. Someone who may have the same problems as them – family, college life, girls, etc. But can also solve crimes. He's a mastermind that no one knows about.'

'Ya, so completely like everything we've seen.'

'Where? Where have you seen such a character?'

'So many TV shows in America.'

'Dude we live in India. Think Indian!'

'India is like single malt. You need to drink it several times to understand that it's not just regular liquor. Know what I mean?'

I didn't. He continued, 'A man always has condoms, lighter and a mobile at hand. Because you never know when you're gonna need all three. Know what I mean?' I stared at him blankly. But he didn't seem to care that I had no idea what he was talking about. It would one of many Kurkurisms that nobody would understand but would go around the office. It was his way of trying to say something that would distract from the fact that he didn't know what the right answer was.

Another one he used as advice to the boys in office was, 'The best asset you have is a smile and if you have yellow teeth, go with a magic trick up your sleeve. Know what I mean?'

No man took his advice but the women seemed to be buying it. Pretty soon we saw him leaving on a lunch dates with women from various departments. Obviously whatever he was saying was charming the pants off ladies who had only given me dirty looks till now. Not only had he stolen my promotion, he had taken over as the new ladies man. A title I was hoping to get one day. I mean, once Radha was out of my life.

It was finally the day to present my Feluda idea. A full two weeks after New Year's Eve. With Radha still in my house and Kurkure as my boss, I had no hope left in anything anymore. I just wanted to get this over with.

33

The entire programming and marketing team were sitting in the board room, as were Tweedledee, Tweedledum and Nincompoop. In walked Kurkure, smelling like he had used the entire contents of the latest Armani perfume. His white shirt was slightly open, revealing strains of yellow hair that were obviously bleached.

Kurkure stood at the head of the table and started the deck I had made for everyone. 'All right guys, I know I'm new here, but I want to tell you how honoured I am to be presenting this great idea to you. Felu, the young, closeted gay Sherlock Holmes.'

'What!' I shouted out. 'That's not what I have written.'

'Now, now Obro, let him speak,' Nincompoop said.

Kurkure smiled and shot me a dirty look. 'We won't make him obviously gay, otherwise we'll lose our audience. But we will gain a new audience of closeted homosexuals if we hint at this subject through this character.'

'I don't agree! Let's stick to the original story,' I interjected.

Kurkure carried on, oblivious to my protests. 'A man's moustache is his identity. Not his girth, mirth or personality. Know what I mean?'

Everyone in the room tittered. Clearly they thought he was incredible amusing. I was boiling in my corner. He continued, 'I've gone through Obro's presentation and I think it was good. I have made some major adjustments and made it great. Let him present it to you. The platform is yours, Master Obro.'

Made adjustments, my ass. Everything was exactly as I had done it. I went through the entire presentation – the characters, the sets and dialogues, the marketing plan. I wrapped up with suggesting we find a new face for the role of Feluda. The presentation had taken thirty minutes, and everyone looked very happy with my work. Except Kurkure got all the credit!

'Excellent job, Kris,' Nincompoop said. 'You've made remarkable progress in such a short time.'

Hello! And what was I? The donkey he rode on?

Finally, Tweedledee said, 'Let's give a big hand to Obro as well, for helping Kris.' And my colleagues who had seen me working late nights and early mornings sat there and didn't say a word in my defence.

But that's how the corporate world is. The man with the least amount of brains or vision is at the senior-most post, making the maximum money. The rest of us who slog away and actually have any brains are never paid enough. And we all think, there's recession, at least we have our jobs. So we never take the chance to stand up for ourselves, quit or look for another job. For those who try, they see that the situation is the same everywhere. Same bad bosses, long hours and no work-life balance. A known devil is always better than an unknown one, we think. We become comfortable in one office. We have a few friends, the IT guy becomes our pal, and the canteen boys sneak cigarettes in for us. We think that for the pay, our life is still better than what it could be outside. So we stay in the same dead-end jobs for years, till we are pushed out by girlfriends or spouses who demand more from us, and only then do we go looking for something else.

I thought I would make television history with Feluda, but Kurkure had come and made falooda out of my idea.

The year had not begun well at all.

34

I tried to speak to Nincompoop, but he said that I should try and accept the new angle. After all, he said, Kris had worked in the TV industry abroad, and management wanted to take this channel to a global level. So, with deep resignation, I left the budgets and details to Kurkure to take forward. I had done my job as asked by Nincompoop. I was also left alone by Tweedledee, who stopped taking me on his evening rounds. But since I didn't want to go back home to Radha, I began to spend more time in the office.

One day, when I was feeling truly low, a girl came up to me. 'Hey,' she said.

I looked up and nodded.

'I've designed the packaging for the Feluda series. Do you want to see it?'

I felt a tingle of excitement in my heart. Maybe the idea had gone awry, but packaging could save the show. After all, that was what drew people in the first place. The content always came later.

'Sure,' I said.

She held out her hand and said, 'I'm Meera.'

I shook her hand, and honestly, I can say there were

electric sparks. Maybe because I hadn't actually touched anyone but Radha for the last two years, such an innocuous gesture sent shivers down my spine. But what she showed me in the edit machine was even more spine-tingling.

'Meera, this is amazing. You've grasped the gist of the character so well!' I said, and went through the entire packaging at least seven times, I was so excited.

'Thanks,' she said smiling. And then, as an afterthought, 'You know you're not as bad as Anu made you out to be.'

I put both my hands on my head and sighed deeply, 'That was such an unfortunate incident. I don't know what I said, but I never meant to hurt anyone. I'm just so bad at talking to girls and dealing with relationships.'

I couldn't believe I was saying this to someone. Was the stress of the last two years making me spout some senti shit? Was I becoming a woman? OMG!

'Look, it's not so complicated. Just be yourself. Don't try to impress anyone, like that asshole Kurkure does.'

My ears pricked up. This was the first person who had said anything negative about him. I raised one eyebrow and said, 'Tell me more.'

She came and sat next to me. 'Well, for starters, he has spent barely any time in the US and he thinks he's Obama's brother. He loves to dance and apparently teaches salsa! He's run a few marathons. He even almost conquered Mt. Everest but gave up at the summit to help a poor Sherpa who was struggling. There's nothing that guy hasn't done.'

'Well that should make him a perfect catch for any woman.'

She shook her head and replied after some time, 'There's something amiss about him. As if he's trying too hard. Is dancing a way to meet girls? And if he takes every woman out, then no woman feels special. But it's also probably because every woman he's taken out has turned him down.'

'What?!'

'Ya. No woman really wants to date him. They like talking to him because he's so different from the rest of the men in this office who are so self-centred and self-absorbed. At least Kurkure has varied interests and is fun to talk to. But when it comes to anything physical with him, we've all made him our "brother". He doesn't have that X factor. It's what women like.'

I was now beaming. She was burying my nemesis. But what did she mean I was self-absorbed? And I went ahead and asked her precisely that. How was it so easy to talk to this woman? Was she from another planet?

'Well I don't know you, but you're only into your work. So if you go up to someone instead of saying, "Hi, how's your day going", you and all the other men here probably ask about work saying, "Hey you have to do this". Or you will hit on the woman and say, "*Kya maal lag rahi hai*, dinner *pe chalegi*". And honestly women aren't flattered by being called that and will never have dinner with you, much less a coffee.'

'I don't say that,' I muttered, wondering if I had ever approached women in that manner. 'So what should one do then?'

Meera smiled at me and said, 'Aren't you already in a relationship? You trying to cheat on her or something?'

I shook my head vigorously, 'Not at all. I've been trying to get out of this toxic relationship but I haven't succeeded at all. I used to love her but I am so unsure now.'

Meera nodded her head sympathetically. 'The only way to get a woman to leave is by finding a way for her to go.'

I looked at her blankly. She continued, 'Make it easy for her to go on her own accord.'

'How do I do that?'

'Let's go outside and smoke. I think better after a *sutta*.'

What a cool woman, I thought. Not only was she giving me relationship advice, she wanted to share a cigarette with me! We walked to the balcony and she gently put her hand on my arm, giving me shivers down my spine. I would totally fantasize about her tonight.

'I have an idea,' she said after a few puffs.

'Wow, your brain really does work after smoking,' I acknowledged.

'I know, right? So – why don't you get to know Kurkure better,' she started before I interrupted her.

'Why would I do that? I already hate the man.'

'Just listen. Get to know him better and start doing the things he does. It intrigues women in the beginning but turns them off eventually. It could work with your girlfriend if you became him! You could repel her the way he repels women.'

The idea didn't seem bad. I could use Kurkure's mannerisms to get ahead in the company and remove Radha from my life.

'It's worth a shot,' I said, and Meera smiled. I looked at her carefully in the sunlight. She had short jet black hair, piercing brown eyes and an easygoing smile. She wore a black jacket with the buttons open over a pink tank top that showed off her curves beautifully. Her jeans were worn in but fit snugly around her hips and thighs. Somehow, I knew her advice would set me free but I didn't know how. For now, I was glad that I had found a friend in the office who seemed to understand me.

35

Making Radha fall out of love with me was tough. It might have been easy for Kurkure, but once a woman has set her heart on Obro, it is mighty difficult to let go!

But the mission of how to figure out breaking up with my clingy girlfriend was underway. I had to Become Kurkure to Get Rid of Radha!

Following Meera's advice, I started hanging out with Kurkure. He was a bumbling, over-confident idiot. Much like most of my cousins. His little cabin (which rightfully should have been mine) was filled with photos of himself doing great things, running the marathon in different places, going on a hot air balloon over the Andes mountains, rappelling in Niagara falls, doing the salsa with a beautiful Puerto Rican.

'She was my guru. Very hot. We had a night of incredible passion. A man's libido cannot be contained within the four walls of a country. Know what I mean?' he said, as I looked at all the photos carefully, wondering how Photoshop had taken over all our lives. It was so obvious that the pictures were as fake as the man, but no one seemed to take notice of it.

Step one of Plan BKGRR (Be Kurkure, Get Rid of Radha)

– take photos of yourself doing great things and stash them away in different places where Radha can find them and question you about them. Casually say you used to do all those things before you met her. She'll soon figure out she's holding you back from your dreams and leave. Also tell her how you were with another woman before her, who was hotter than she is. She'll die of jealousy or spend sleepless nights wondering how she can be better.

A week later I planted a few photos of myself climbing a mountain and kayaking in Iceland, photos that I had taken on a green screen in a studio and spent precious office hours all through Monday to Friday photoshopping. Radha found them and said, 'Did you do all this?'

I smirked. Bye bye, baby! 'Ya.'

'It looks fake.'

'It's not fake.' I said indignantly. 'It was before I met you. I had a rocking life.'

'You had no life before you met me. Even so, I'm so glad you finished doing all these dangerous things before you met me. Because now I wouldn't let you go anywhere without me. And the only mountain that we'll see is through our window in the Swiss Alps in Gstaad where Kareena Kapoor and Saif Ali Khan go for *their* vacations.'

Bloody Bollywood!.

When I went back and told Meera that my plan had failed, she laughed her head off and said, 'You should actually learn to do something rather than pretend you did it. Why don't you take up a hobby like he did?'

So I went back to find out what hobbies he was interested in besides dancing. No self-respecting man dances well unless he has taken some classes. We all have two left feet. The only reason why a man learns how to dance like a dream, is to pick up chicks. No. I wasn't learning salsa.

I had to figure out other ways that Kurkure was annoying to women.

Step two of Plan BKGRR – I would use his Kukureisms with Radha.

For a few days in a row, I started saying absurd things at home, and acting like a complete dude in front of her. 'Hey, Radha. Do you want to get a DTH connection? Coz if you can't tape it, you can't roll with it. Know what I mean?'

'Yes I do. Good idea. I'll call some DTH guys tomorrow and ask them to talk to you.'

Or I would say, 'Hey Radha, I don't think I want to keep this maid anymore. What you can't do yourself, ain't worth doin'. Know what I mean?'

Radha turned around, put her hands on her hips and said, 'Fine. I think you should do the dishes from tomorrow.'

'No no no no no. I only meant how much is she charging? I mean, can we find someone cheaper?'

None of the fine Kurkuresims were working at home with my girlfriend. I had to find another way to repulse her.

Step three of Plan BKGRR – dye my hair blond!

I went to the parlour after work one day and asked for streaks in my hair. When I heard how much it would cost I had a mini heart attack.

'Would you like some ice tea and donuts while you get your service done?' The gentle lady manager asked. I thought, why not. I had to find a way to get rid of Radha. And I might as well eat to compensate for the amount I was spending for this.

At the end of one-and-a-half hours, I had blond streaks in

my hair and had eaten twelve donuts that were now making me feel very sick.

But when I went home I was sure one look and Radha would leave me. She would be horrified that I had changed myself into this clown. I prepared myself for a huge meltdown about how she liked the old Obro and the new look was making her sick. I walked in and Radha was watching TV. For a woman who claimed she read a lot, I'd hardly ever seen her with a book.

One look at me and she squealed. This was it. She was leaving. Bye bye, Radha. 'I love it!'

Huh?

'You look so sexy! You look like a new man. I have fallen in love with you all over again.'

She threw her arms around me and gave me a passionate kiss. And I got so aroused that we ended up in bed for a full ten minutes. This was not what I had planned, but a man has to go with the flow in certain situations. 'Know what I mean?'

Clearly my attempt in becoming Kurkure was failing. I had to think of a new plan.

When I went back to Meera to show her my new look, she burst out laughing. 'Dude, I would definitely leave you! You look hilarious.'

Instead of feeling better, I felt a little snubbed. I gave her a weak smile and left the Smoke studio where she was working.

What was happening? Was I falling for Meera? While I was living with Radha? And trying to imitate Kurkure? I had to figure out what was going on inside my head. I decided to call the one person who knew me better than I knew myself. I knew I would be sorted out then.

36

'Ma,' I said into the receiver. 'What was Baba like when he married you?'

'What kind of a question is this? Horlicks *kheyecho*?'

'*Haan* Ma. I've had Horlicks today.'

'*Thanda legegache.* Muffler *poro ni*? (You've got a cold. You didn't wear a muffler?)'

This was useless. Obviously, my mother and I had grown so far apart that she didn't know her son was going through troubled times. And I could never speak to my father. Even when we were young he only had one thing to say to us: 'Where's your mother?' And if we ever asked him something, he would reply, 'Go ask your mother.'

As soon as she was convinced I was not ill, my mother began prattling on and on about how her sister would win if Lengtu got married before me. And wouldn't I just come home once to see some girls?

'I can't Ma. And I don't want to get married right now. How many times have I told you this?'

'Well why don't you just get engaged and make me happy? You know I'm not getting younger and my dying wish is to see you settled with a woman of my choice...I mean a woman who makes you happy.'

'You're not dying, Ma. And you have plenty of years left in you. Tell me, what is Tumpa Mashi up to?' And my mother suddenly had someone to gossip about so the topic of my marriage was dropped.

Suddenly, I missed home terribly. I hadn't been back in so long. The fun and excitement of youth is best in your home town. Where people knew you and you didn't have to worry so much. These last three years had gone by in a blur and it was time I made a decision about my life. Did I want to stay in Mumbai or go back home to Kolkata? Maybe it was time that I quit and left. After all, I wasn't getting anywhere at work.

But destiny has other plans. Every time you think you've made a decision about a certain situation, she'll throw in a few surprises just to confuse you.

I was at my desk doing the *Mid-Day* puzzle, when I heard some shouting coming from Nincompoop's office. I looked towards the commotion and saw Kurkure slowly skulk out from the cabin. Nincompoop saw me looking at him and shouted for me. 'Come here!'

I quickly put down the newspaper and rushed over to his room.

Nincompoop was furious at Kurkure. Apparently they'd done a survey to see how people would receive the show as Kurkure had envisaged it. And no one had approved of Feluda being a closet homosexual at all. Nincompoop raved and ranted and said I needed to save the show. He wanted to go back to the original ideas we had for the character.

I was super thrilled. I would be leading the project again! Maybe this was a sign from the universe to not give up just yet. Maybe I would stay in Mumbai till this show went on air. I would gauge what to do with my career post that.

I exited the office only to see Kurkure go off with Anu for lunch. How did that man do it? Anu, who hated me simply for having lunch with her and not telling her I had a girlfriend, was dating this blond-streaked, US-returned Richard Simmons. Honestly, I don't know what women see in some men. Or what they want from regular men. They will always fall for the bizarre, bad boy rather than the simple, normal guy. They'll put words in the mouth of us men who can't express themselves so well, and twist it till we're hung out to dry, and take what a bad boy says in the most decent manner as if he's born from a holy spirit. It's unfair. Made relationships even more complicated and men more confused.

I got back to work on my project and before I knew it an hour had passed and Kurkure was back.

I looked at him and said sarcastically, 'The boss screams at you and you go out for lunch?'

He replied, 'A man is only defeated when he can't drink anymore. He's never beaten if a boss makes him sore. Know what I mean?'

I hardly cared. I had got my pet project back and was on top of the world. Kurkure went to the bathroom and Menon came up to me. 'Hey man.'

'What up, yo!'

Menon shook his head and said, 'Dude, why are you trying to become like the ass of the office?'

'What?' I didn't understand. I thought Kurkure was the envy of every man. I did remember what Meera had said about him, but I had thought that all the men were jealous of how easily he could interact with women, and his fancy lifestyle abroad.

'Look, doesn't he seem a bit off to you? The way he dresses?

The way he swings his hips as if he's doing the salsa here. The way he only wears jackets? How he only likes drinking wine?'

No. I didn't get it.

'What are you trying to say, Menon?'

'Well if you were hanging out with the boys, you'd know we all think he's gay!'

'What?' I couldn't believe it. I was trying to become a homosexual without realizing it.

'I had to warn you,' Menon continued. 'Why do you think he wanted to make Feluda gay? Coz he relates to it somewhere, bro.'

Shit. And I had been copying him to get rid of Radha. No wonder she was falling for all the charming tricks. Since she already knew my prowess in bed, she just loved the new additional personality.

'What should I do?' I asked Menon.

'Listen, even if he's that, I don't think he's going to go for you. He's more of a cool type. So you can relax.'

For several minutes after Menon left I was wondering if he had just advised me or offended me. I needed Meera's help with this one. But I needed to talk to her with my poker face. I couldn't show her I was falling in love with her. And I knew if I displayed even a little bit of emotion, the woman would fall at my feet. After all, I was irresistible to anyone of the female species.

37

I was walking towards the editing machines where Meera worked, when Anu came up to me and said, 'Hey Obro. How are you?'

I almost flipped over and died.

I stopped in my tracks and didn't say a word. She continued, 'I know I gave you a hard time and I'm sorry about it.'

I was puzzled. Was a woman apologizing? I looked around. Was this a prank? Was I on TV? Was I being Punked?

I was stunned. No woman in the history of time, since the Big Bang theory, had ever apologized to a man. They were incapable of admitting they were wrong. When two women fought, they would ignore each other for the rest of their lives, instead of saying how sorry they were. And a woman never apologized to a man because she always believed she was a superior creature who didn't need to belittle herself and her intelligence in front of a lesser mortal. Even Eve in the garden of Eden, after eating the apple, tempted by the serpent, and causing the fall of man, would have blamed her better half: 'It was all because you weren't paying attention to me. So I had to bite that apple. It's your fucking fault.'

So my first question to her was, 'Are you serious?'

Anu nodded. I sighed in relief, 'I'm so sorry too, Anu. I should have told you; I'm a complete idiot. Hope we can be friends.'

Hell, a man has to take his chances, and if there's one thing I've learnt on how to pick up women, it is to apologize profusely. It makes women melt and feel they're superior to you, they must teach you the correct way, and from the bottom of their benevolent heart, give you another chance.

'Did you have a fun lunch with Kurkure?' I asked her.

'Oh that dufus! He's barely got a degree.'

'How do you know?' I asked. The story about Kurkure was getting murkier and murkier.

'I could guess. I put all the things he told me together and realized that he didn't have a job for the longest time. And that he met Nincompoop in a bar where they did salsa together.'

Was Nincompoop also gay? Was he keeping Kurkure at a distance because he didn't want anyone to find out his true identity? Did Kurkure have pictures of them together that he was blackmailing Nincompoop with? This office politics was getting more and more complicated. Thank God I still had a job.

'Why do so many women go out with him then? What's wrong with the rest of us?'

'He is easy to be with.'

'How?'

'He doesn't push too hard. With the least effort he's most charming. Girls like that.'

I began to think about how men could get women with the least amount of effort. What would it take to win a woman over?

Here we go again. I should be paid separately for these 'Notes for Dummies', you know. I am like a Cool Guru.

Five Ways to Win a Woman Over and Make it Look Easy!

1. Appear comfortable. Not only should you be cool and confident when you enter a room, you should be comfortable in your surroundings. Holding a drink at a party and slinking into one corner is not going to help you. Move around the room / office with or without a drink and talk to everyone. Kurkure made it a point to speak to every girl.

2. Seem attentive. Ask questions with genuine interest. Listen to what the girl is saying about her life. Appear sympathetic. The more she talks the more she wants to impress you. All you have to do is nod and smile and say, 'Is that so? How did you feel about that?'

3. Make the date. Kurkure started with – 'I'm new here and I promise to buy you lunch if you help me with this one little thing.' Obviously it was a small thing and then he would say – 'I insist on getting you lunch.' Hence a date was set.

4. Know a joke. Find great jokes and know how to use them in the right situations. Office jokes are great if you know the equations there. But making fun of your boss' girlfriend might backfire. Don't use a pick-up line. A joke is different. And the stale ones of once a Hindu, a Jew and a buffalo walked into a bar are old. Be 'with it'.' Once you make a girl smile, you'll have a few more minutes to convince her that she should go on a date with you.

5. Personal history. Has any aunt died in your family? I

know, it sounds cheap, but women love sentimental stuff. Keeping a picture of an old woman on your desk might elicit some conversation. 'She raised me from when I was a child. Was devastated when she passed away a few months ago. Still haven't got over that. She was the one who showed me how to respect women. Finest lesson I've ever learnt.' Boom! The girl will spend five more minutes talking to you.

'Anyway,' Anu continued, 'let me know if you want any help with the marketing. I have a few ideas.'

'Sure,' I said. 'Let's discuss this over coffee at four?' She nodded and went back to her seat.

Too many thoughts were spinning in my head. Anu was in love with me! Meera wanted me. Radha was living with me. Kurkure and Nincompoop were probably gay. I had dyed my hair blond.

Know what I mean?

38

So I dreamt of a foursome. This is the highest a man can go in a dream. I was in bed with Anu, Meera and Radha doing all sorts of naughty things to me. The fact that I had all these three women in my life and I still hadn't had sex in days was ironic. No wonder I was having dreams, and was working on lists like this:

Ten Facts About Men (That Even Men Don't Know)

This piece was written so you can show it to your girlfriend. But don't expect sex after she reads it.

1. Men evaluate each other by the four pillars of success: cars, watches, mobile phones and chicks. Even if they live in a rundown place, you will never see it because men don't go to each other's houses (unless the spouse invites couples over, and that's because women like to show off their domestic skills – how they've decorated the place, their hostess skills, the nice curtains, and all such dainty stuff). Men always meet at bars. Men can be best friends forever (something women don't have the luxury of saying), and never see each other's homes. If a woman is not invited to her

best friend's house, she becomes suspicious and they will have a fight.

2. Men are obsessed with cars. We're divided into four different categories here. The Family Man, who buys an economical car with CNG that fits his parents, kids, spouse and dog. The Flashy Man: CEOs and General Morons who like to buy status symbol cars and compare brands with each other (congruous to how big mine is as compared to yours). The Confused Man: he changes his car every month just to show off. Probably rents it out from a high-end car service and doesn't know a thing about them. The Broke Man: has had the same car for the last ten years. Is still paying an EMI and thinks just because he's serviced it recently, he can manage to '*chalao*' it for another year at least, but still looks at other cars with deep desire. As for their wives, they don't really care as long as the driver is there on time.

3. Men never discuss their bank balances. They just show it through the four pillars to create an impact. That's why the hot supermodels chicks are constantly in demand. They make a man look good. If a model wants to be with a guy, it means he's worth some serious money and stature to look after such a high maintenance woman!

4. Men cannot carry off too many accessories. Otherwise they'll look like a 'Bhai', or worse, a girl. Even if they wear designer clothes and designer shoes, they only have to wear an expensive watch, carry the latest mobile or wear a Gucci belt. So most men will wear the same shirt and trousers for years with a worn-out belt, but always have either an expensive watch or a new mobile that they'll put down on the table when they eat just to show off.

5. The watch a man is wearing is either something

sentimental – his father or girlfriend gave it to him – or it's the latest brand that he's gifted himself for his birthday because he think his thirty-first birthday is just super awesome. Or it could be a sporty, underwater watch because he wants to project an image of being cool and a scuba diving instructor. The other men will probably get this image. The women just don't care.

6. Men love sex dreams. The foursome is the best kind. It's not just a threesome. It's three women and you. Out of the two terabyte of porn a man may have, the foursome is a rare combination. Hence the dream is super successful. A man is on a high when he wakes up.

7. Men like staring at themselves in the mirror as much as women do. They like to check out how great their faces look. They never see the pimples, wrinkles, white hair. They compare themselves to the most handsome man in the world. So next time your man asks you if he's better looking than Brad Pitt, just say yes. Coz he believes he is. If you say no, he'll only think you are a moron for not noticing it and try to find a woman who will say yes. Also do let him keep his moustache. He thinks he's a Bollywood hero and all the women are drooling over him because of it.

8. Men like to work out only to enhance their body to get laid. The better their bodies, the more the chicks. Even a pot-bellied man will think he's God's gift to women. Because he went to the gym, did about three-and-a-half minutes on the treadmill, did a few seated rows and carried a two pound bar across his shoulders to show the women there that he was doing side crunches. All of which would have burnt ten calories. Which would have been replaced with the first mouthful of the heavy breakfast he indulges in because it's

the most important meal of the day, and it's essential to have aloo parathas.

9. TV is another important element of a man. Not what they watch, but how big it is. It's the only thing they'll show off when other male members come to their house. A man has arrived in life if he has a projection screen. A 64-inch Full HD 3D plasma shows he's well off. If he has a large TV in every room, it means he's upper middle class. If he has a TV in his bathroom, it means he's 'lucky'. They all need to be plasmas, or at the minimum, LEDs. A man with a large box from the last decade will never invite another man home.

10. Our friends are our life, but our partners are our soul mates. Men hate it when they have to choose between the two. The friends hate the woman we love and the woman hates us spending time with our friends. It makes our life difficult. And in the end we may choose the woman, but we'll harbour a small resentment towards you for the rest of our lives. So let us spend time with our boys when we like and we'll give you what you need. Heck, we don't complain about how much time you spend with your girl friends. Mutual space always makes a relationship work better.

I realized it was Saturday and went back to sleep. I had a full two days to dream about my fabulous women. I wasn't going to get up and ruin it at all. I pulled the pillow over my head and had, for the first time in months, a lovely weekend.

39

The most exciting day of my career had arrived. My idea was going to be executed. Day 1 of the shooting of the Feluda series. I was supposed to oversee everything, and I was extremely excited. I hadn't slept the entire night thinking how much power I had in this company.

I got dressed and was about to leave when Radha entered the bathroom.

'Bye Radha. Wish me best of luck,' I called out, one leg out the door.

I heard her scream and run out holding a towel over herself. Well maybe I could be five minutes late if she really wanted to please me.

'Obro,' she said, looking worried.

'Now, now. Don't worry. I can be a little late. Lighting always takes time. Come. Let's go to the bedroom.'

'Obro!' she said sternly. 'Wait here.' She went inside and came out wearing her stupid Elco Arcade nightie, which was a complete turn-off.

'Obro, I've found a lump on my breast. It looks suspicious,' she said and sat down to cry.

Shit. I forgot about my shoot. I sat down next to her and

said, 'It's okay Radha. I'm with you. I won't go to office today. I'll tell them to go ahead with the shoot without me. Let's head to the hospital.'

'No, no. It's okay. I'll manage. This is important to you. You must go.'

Why do women pose a problem to men and then ask them to not bother while they handle it on their own? Do they not know we are problem-solvers, not conversation-makers? Women love this shit. They have a four-step program to give guilt to men:

1. Pose a problem to the man – 'I'm really sick.' 'The maid has not come.' 'I have had a big fight with my mother.'

2. Convince the man it's not their problem – 'It's okay, I can manage it on my own.' 'It's no concern to you I know.' 'Don't worry, I'll handle it.'

3. Persuade you to continue with your work – 'If the office can't function without you, you must leave.' 'I understand if you can't get out of the meeting.' 'If you have to travel, then go.'

4. Expect you to have done the opposite – 'I didn't think the meeting was more important than me!' 'I feel you neglect me for office ALL the time. It's as if I don't exist.' 'How could you travel when I was going through such a crisis? Do you not get me at all?'

Guilt. The cornerstone of every relationship. The reason men stay in terrible partnerships.

It would be easier if women just saved us the guilt and tell us what they want and how to do it.

So I left. She said she would ask her friend to take her to the hospital and I thought that was a splendid idea. I even told her to 'keep me posted' so I would know what the doctor said even though I had a terribly busy day ahead. She just gave me a dirty look when I left.

Half-way to the shoot, the messages started. Women can never say things to men to their face. They will wait while you're in the middle of something else to bring back something that could have been sorted ten minutes ago if you had only opened your mouth then.

'I can't believe you left me in this state.'

'I will probably have cancer and die and all you can think about is the shoot. I mean nothing to you.'

'I can't believe you'd let my friend take me to the hospital. You didn't even offer.'

'I think we need to talk.'

Everything ends with that. So I turned the bike around and headed home. And just as Radha was leaving with her friend, I caught them. I made Radha get on my bike and took her to the hospital.

I called office and told them I would be taking a sick day. Tweedledee couldn't believe that I wouldn't be there for the first day of shoot. He called me and yelled for half an hour straight; when he paused for breath I told him that I was taking my girlfriend to the doctor because she suspected that, at the age of twenty-five, she had the Big C.

She didn't.

After speaking to the doctor about her choices, she went and got some tests done. I had to use my credit card because it was too expensive to withdraw money from the ATM. I would be paying in EMI for this for the rest of my life. After several hours of hospital corridors, half a day had passed.

The nurse finally came out to see me where I was waiting in the corridor.

'You can go in and see her now.'

'Thank you Sister. Is it...?'

The nurse shook her head and said, 'It was just some ingrown boil. We've removed it. She's fine. You can take her home.'

What!

I walked in and saw Radha had already changed. She said with a smile, 'Did you hear the good news? It wasn't cancer! I'm so relieved.'

She threw her arms around me and kissed me hard. I pulled away.

'You mean to tell me that I missed the most important day of my life for you to get a boil removed?'

'Well we didn't know it was just a boil,' Radha said defensively.

I couldn't believe the tactics my girlfriend would use to cling on to me. To not let me enjoy the greatest day of my life.

I yelled right in the hospital room. 'Radha, I can't believe the *chakkars* you do! What is wrong with you? Didn't you know this day was important to me?'

'I told you to go,' she said.

'And you blackmailed me into coming back!'

'You did that all by yourself. I thought you wanted to be here with me.'

'Because I thought you had a deadly disease!'

'So it would be okay if I *had* a deadly disease but not okay that it was nothing and I'm safe?' she yelled back.

Women twist everything. Instead of apologizing, she made me feel bad all over again.

'I'm sorry,' I started, 'I didn't mean it like that.'

'Well why don't you think about what you really mean

and say that. I just want to go home and forget about this day completely!'

I filled out all the discharge forms and spent every last bit of my money on Radha's hospital visit that she didn't even want to remember.

And on the other hand, I would hear that the shoot went off so superbly that everyone called for beer and pizza on the sets and had a blast as a unit on the first day. I was sorely missed.

40

The more I tried to avoid Kurkure, the more he clung to me for support. After six weeks in office, he had been on a lunch date with every woman once. And no woman twice. No guy was hanging out with him and even though he tried to sweet talk his way back into Tweedledee and Tweedledum's good books, they were too busy plotting to overthrow Nincompoop to take notice of Kurkure. So the only person who was left was me. And being the good soul that I am, I just let him shadow me to see the impact I had on people.

After around three weeks of shooting and editing, we had a bank of ten episodes and were ready to start it on our channel. The channel had been running promos and tickers about Feluda for about two weeks. Hoardings had been put up and media spots bought. A lot of money had been spent on my idea. If it worked, I would be a big name. And if it flopped, I would need to pack up and leave for Kolkata forever.

'Hey guys,' Tweedledee said one evening, 'tomorrow night is the launch of Feluda. Let's all watch it here in the evening and then go out for drinks after that!'

A huge wave of cheers roared through the office. We

deserved this. We had been working hard. Kurkure smiled and turned to me and said, 'It will be nice for all of us to hang out on Valentine's Day. Who knows, maybe after a few drinks Meera will go out with me again.'

Shit! Valentine's Day! I had completely forgotten about it. And every woman expects something on Valentine's Day. I swear it was a day invented by some stupid woman to again test the man to see if he truly loves her. And red roses, a candlelight dinner and an expensive present are the true symbols of this test. It didn't matter if the poor sod bought flowers ALL year round; if he didn't do it on February 14, he was doomed.

I went back home that day and Radha was in a foul mood. 'The cook left,' she said as she dug into a bag of chips.

'I thought she'd left long ago. I thought you were cooking.'

'I can't believe you know so little about your own house. No. That was the cleaning bai. And I found another woman to replace her. How much I do for you!'

I didn't want to tell her that she was the one who was sitting at home the entire day and if she wanted she could easily cook and then clean the house and save me four thousand rupees!

'Anyway, I don't want to cook tomorrow so I hope you've planned something nice.'

I put down my laptop bag and said, 'About that...'

She looked at me sternly, 'Now don't tell me that you won't be here for Valentine's Day. You've been so busy the entire month and I haven't said anything.'

Hogwash. She had refused to give me food when I came home on several occasions because I was late. She had been the opposite of understanding. I should actually punish her by not being there tomorrow. In fact, we weren't even officially a couple. She had broken up with me before New Year's Eve and just because we had sex one night didn't mean we were back together. Did it?

'Actually, I have another idea. Everyone is going to watch the first Feluda episode in office and then go out drinking. Why don't you join us?' My super-brain had suddenly come up with a genius plan. Instead of paying for her drinks and dinner, I would just let her tag along with us, and the company would have to pay for it. No boss would refuse a woman on Valentine's Day.

'But I thought we could go out together, alone,' she said, sounding diffident.

'It'll be fun. You'll meet all my friends at work.' Oh please let it work!

'Okay. I guess introducing me to all your friends is also a way of showing love.'

'Yes it is.' And the plan was set.

The next day the entire office was abuzz. I was on tenterhooks. This was a make or break time for me. Radha came to office at sharp seven in the evening as I had asked her to. Half an hour before the show, I was called in for a meeting so I asked Kurkure to take her to the canteen for a cup of coffee.

It was finally time. The entire office gathered around the large TV set in Nincompoop's office. I sat next to Tweedledee while Kurkure took care of Radha, who was standing next to him. I was thankful that she hadn't asked to sit next to me or had a crisis at the time.

The next half hour passed by in a haze. Feluda was received with a standing ovation. Everyone seemed to love it.

The IT chap who was monitoring the Twitter, Facebook and other social media sites to see the response said that it was trending. I was so glad and relieved to hear this. I had done it. I had succeeded in doing something for myself. I had arrived in Mumbai and I could now say I had a reason to stay.

Everyone headed out to Toto's, to celebrate. Kurkure, Radha, Meera and I managed to get a table and sat down. The fun was about to begin.

41

I was on a high with the response to the Feluda show. That's why I didn't see the signs. The signs that something was brewing and a new relationship was about to start. Something that would leave me extremely confused.

'Tequila shots!' Tweedledee called out, and we all agreed. After the shot and a drink each, everyone was quite buzzed. We joked about the scenes in Feluda. We laughed about the tough few weeks we'd all had. We made fun of our boss and Radha was sweet enough to laugh along.

Then the girls had to go the bathroom. Yes, together. I honestly don't know why women always go to the loo together, but they do. No man has ever said, 'Dude I need to take a piss, you coming?' The other man would probably look at him and say, 'Are you fuckin' kidding me?' Of course, after you are punch drunk, it's a different tale.

Kurkure turned to me once the girls had left and said, 'Radha is really special. She's so smart and beautiful.'

I nodded and joked, 'You want her?'

And suddenly he became grave and said, 'Dude seriously?' And for a moment I wondered if he was testing how much I loved her, or whether he truly wanted Radha. But what about what Menon had said about him being gay? I would find out later. Just then he laughed and said, 'Meera's flirting with you big time!'

'What?'

I hadn't even noticed.

'Ya. She's into you. I wouldn't be surprised if they're having a cat fight in the women's restroom about who's going to get you.'

I laughed out loud. 'You're mad. We're just friends. And Radha would kill me if I even looked at anyone else.'

He took a sip of his beer and shrugged. 'I'm just telling you, man.'

Before I could say anything, the girls came back. Radha sat next to me but she was facing Kurkure and suddenly I saw that she was looking at him in a strange way. Meera seemed extremely chilled and asked for a round of beer for us. She started speaking about the next episode's packaging with me, and Radha pulled out her phone.

While Meera and I talked about scenes and music, I saw that Radha and Kurkure were busy on their phones. I turned to Radha and said, 'I'm sorry that we're boring you, darling. Meera, no more chatting about work till tomorrow. I don't want Radha to play games while we're here.'

'Oh, don't worry. I just want to finish this conversation with my friend. She's having some problems. I'll just be back.' Radha got up and walked out of the restaurant to make a phone call.

A few seconds later, Kurkure excused himself to go to the restroom. Meera and I were left alone.

'So,' she said leaning forward. 'That plan of yours to get rid of Radha seems to be working.'

I laughed heartily and said, 'Yes. Since she has stuck to me the entire night after three drinks and really hasn't said a word.'

'Oh I thought that was your plan. Kurkure is gonna rock it!'

'What?' I was aghast. Where was this coming from? Was I so buzzed that I couldn't see Kurkure hitting on my girlfriend? And was Meera just saying that to get into my pants? I mean, it was a Bengal tiger in there after all.

Meera explained it to me better, 'Look, this is a great chance for you. Let her go. Let Kurkure charm her. And later if she comes back to you, say you can't take betrayal. It's the only thing a woman understands as a reason for a man to break up with her. And if she's happy with him, then good for her.'

Kurkure and Radha came back almost simultaneously. The rest of the evening, and as Radha and I headed home, Meera's words swirled in my head. All the way back in the cab, she was texting someone. I asked her who she was chatting with, and she said again that it was just her friend who was going through a crisis. Now I would have bought this story had it not been for Meera who had planted a strange thought in my brain.

So at night when Radha had gone to sleep, I did what I had never done before and what Radha does every night to me. I checked her phone. There were no text messages or Whatsapp messages. None. She had deleted everything. I put it down and went to the bathroom. When I returned her phone was blinking. I picked it up and checked. Radha had not been chatting with her friend. Apparently she had a mini crisis of her own.

Radha had been chatting with Kurkure. He had fallen in love with her. And she was wondering how to be with him without hurting my feelings.

Meera was right. Now I didn't know what to do. On the one hand I didn't want Radha in my life, but on the other, I felt betrayed and hurt. How could she cheat on me? After all I'd done for her. Sometimes it's best that a person doesn't know why the relationship ends. The betrayal could kill a man's confidence. And right now I was feeling very confused about the entire situation.

42

'Are you kidding? This is great news,' Lengtu said on the phone the following day. I'd called him on my way to work from a dhaba where I'd stopped to have a cup of tea and an egg sandwich. 'Now you're free to be with whomever you want.'

'But I don't have anyone in my life. Who will look after the house? My clothes? My food?' I whined.

Lengtu wasn't hearing any of it. 'You can always come back home. Your mother will do it. In the meantime, go bang as many girls as you can so that once you're back you can get into an arranged marriage.'

'What?'

'You don't think you'll get away so easily, do you? Girls will be lined up and you'll have to pick one. Welcome to my world, Pantha!'

I knew what he was saying was correct. But now was not the time to worry about an arranged marriage. I had to figure out what to do with Radha.

'I feel this sense of betrayal though,' I said, trying to talk about my feelings to Lengtu.

'Hang on. Let me get Nandu. All this senti nonsense you can tell her.'

My cousin Nandini gave me some solid advice, 'Dada, if you're sure Kurkure is in love with her, let her go. She'll be happier. And if he isn't, it's time to move on anyway. You can't stay in a dead-end relationship just because you have history. Don't you remember all the things she's done to you?'

Yes, I did remember what she had done to me. But I also remembered what she had done *for* me. And I didn't want her to be unhappy. I also felt slighted. Kurkure could have just asked me if things were okay between Radha and me before he made his move on her. Not go behind my back. So I asked Kurkure in an indirect manner what he really thought about Radha.

'She's lovely. Ethereal. Just like a woman should be. You're damn lucky, dude.'

He did seem truly in love with her. I should have been glad, but I was puzzled. Then he said something that blew my mind away. 'What are you going to do about Meera though? She's completely into you. Two women! Now that's a mess.'

'Are you crazy?' I said. 'Meera is not into me. She's a friend. And Radha seems to be into someone else. So it isn't two women. It's *no* women in my life.'

Kurkure smiled and said, 'You may not see it, but everyone knows that Meera likes you. You should give her a chance.'

I looked at him and said, 'So you can have a chance with Radha?'

That hit him like a ton of bricks. I continued, 'Yes. I know all about the messaging you were doing with her. I saw all of them.' I hadn't but he didn't need to know that.

Kurkure's jaw fell to the floor. 'Look Obro, I didn't mean...'

'You didn't mean to steal my woman?'

'It's not like that.'

'Like what? You want to pass Meera on to me so you can have Radha?'

'Look man, you can't have one hand in your pocket and another in a cookie jar. Know what I mean?'

I thought that was an extremely rude thing to say and I did what any self-respecting man would do. I hit him. Bengalis aren't fighters. We're peace-loving folk who only want to sit with a pipe in front of the TV and drink our whiskey quietly. But when Bengalis are pushed into a corner, there's a revolution that no one can contain!

Kurkure pounced on me. We started fighting and everyone came out to watch. Now here's the thing when men fight. No one really wants to break it up unless they absolutely have to. They don't want to get into a mess. Also it's great fun to watch. It distracts them from the boring routine of whatever they are doing to see other people mess up their bodies and lives. It's the best reality show ever. Menon even filmed us. Later it would go viral on YouTube. It wasn't because I fight like a girl. It was because I cursed in Bengali. '*Suorer bachcha.*' '*Gadha.*' '*Boka choda!*' No one takes me seriously unless I curse.

Finally Tweedledee broke us up and made us wash up. A doctor was called in to look at our hands and face and patch us up. Meera had been watching the entire episode. She locked eyes with me for a moment and then walked away.

I followed her when no one was looking and found her in the Smoke machine room.

'Meera,' I said softly as I entered. 'I'm sorry you had to see that. Kurkure was saying shit about you and I–'

Suddenly Meera got up and kissed me. I was spellbound.

It was the most delicious kiss I've ever had. It felt like the first time I had kissed Radha. Suddenly I realized that what Kurkure was saying about Meera was true. She was into me.

'That was the hottest thing I've ever seen, Obro. And it was so unexpected. I didn't think you had it in you,' she murmured as she pulled away. Maybe Meera had been helping me get rid of Radha because she wanted me to herself! How sneaky, and so hot.

Now I had two women in my life and I didn't know what to do with either of them.

Did I want to break up with Radha? What did Meera want from me? I had to go home and sort out my head.

43

'Radha, we need to talk,' I said as I got home. She looked at me and became extremely quiet. 'Shall I get you something?' she asked.

'Tea.'

She brought me tea while I composed myself. I had been sent home early after Nincompoop called me into his office and said a committee would look into the matter; if it came to that, I might be suspended. So now I would not have a job and I would have to move back to Kolkata all because of Radha messaging her newly-acquired boyfriend which made me get into a fight with him.

She came back with an ice pack for my head and hand and some hot tea and a chicken sandwich. Women can be this sweet only when they've done something wrong.

'I know what you are up to. Tell me the truth,' I said as I ate the sandwich hungrily before she took it away or threw it across the room in a fit.

'What do you mean?' she asked innocently. Women will always play the 'dumb' card when they're guilty. Most of the time it works because the man has no proof of what she's done. He just suspects and accuses. Unlike a woman who will get hard evidence and then confront the man so she will end up with a solitaire if they get back together, or clean out his bank account if she chooses to walk out.

'I know there's something going on between you and Kurkure. It's the reason I pounded him today, which might make me lose my job.'

Radha was quiet for a moment, then she said, 'I'm sorry Obro. It was a lapse in judgement. I messaged him but I truly love you. How noble of you to fight for me.'

What? How did this happen? It wasn't noble. I just had pent-up anger that came out. He had taken my job. Then he had taken my girl. Then he had said things about my relationship with Meera, which actually turned out to be true, so the reason why I started the fight was really just my fault.

But here I was stuck with Radha once again! Nandini had said if I confront her she would be sorry and leave. But she wanted me even more. It had to be my rakish charm that I had so many women in my life. I remained quiet. And then I thought to myself that while it may be comfortable to have Radha around in my life, I needed some adventure. Radha and I had broken up and got back together so many times that we knew how the story would end. With us being a bitter old couple if we didn't take the step now to move forward in separate directions.

'Radha, you don't love me. If you did you would never want to be with someone else.'

'That's not true. Sometimes we get so bored in relationships that we need a little excitement outside. It doesn't mean we let go of that relationship,' she tried to reason with me.

'Probably, but our relationship isn't just about boredom. We've grown apart. Maybe you're right. Maybe this relationship was over last year and we have just dragged it out.'

Radha sat very still and didn't say a word. Finally, after several minutes, she spoke up. 'You're right,' she said.

Her voice startled me, and I had no idea what she was talking about. Because by now my mind had wandered into another territory. Bikes. If I became single I would definitely buy a better bike. I knew which one I wanted. The Royal Enfield Continental. Oooh, what a bike. I was going to go tomorrow and do a test ride.

'You're so right,' Radha said emphatically to something I had said. I could not believe that finally, after two years, I had got the woman to agree to something I'd said and I had forgotten what it was!

'Huh?' I asked.

'You're right. We *have* grown apart.' Aah. Back to the same topic. I thought it was over. I had said what I needed to. End of discussion. Why do women like dragging a conversation out? Especially when it's about their relationships. It's the easiest one for men to have. Either you're in or you're out.

So we broke up. It was as simple as that. All it takes is another man in a woman's life for her to get over a relationship. Women truly can never be single. They have to have one foot in the door before they completely lock themselves out of another. *Know what I mean?*

~

In two weeks I was out of the house. And Kurkure had moved in. I had nowhere to go. So much for him being gay. He was truly a metrosexual man who oozed charm and could woo women. Menon and the guys had been so wrong. Just because you're macho and rough doesn't make you a man. I learnt from Kurkure that you could also be caring and sensitive and get the woman. Sometimes.

I proposed to Meera with one of my pick-up lines. She laughed at me. Soon after she found another job in a rival channel and left without ever looking back. I was broken-hearted for about five minutes till Menon took me out for a drinking session.

Just then the high and mighty 'Judgement Committee' (a group of fuck-all people who sit around a room the entire day and deliberate on the fuck-all attitudes of the people in the organization and how they can change it and never see the irony in their own fucked name – JC) came back with a verdict on my fight with Kurkure.

They suspended him and kept me. My Feluda story was a big hit and I was an asset to the company. But I didn't have a home. So I made a decision.

I quit.

44

I wanted to prove myself in Mumbai and I had. I had made a fantastic show that everyone loved and I had been vindicated in my fight against Kurkure. I had fallen in love, looked after a woman for two years and never been unfaithful. I had a woman hit on me and had a mad fling with her for exactly five minutes. Life was complete! I was ready to go home to my parents and be looked after. I packed up my bags and took the next flight home. For good. Ready to start a new life. Alone and jobless.

~

We used to live on the corner of Lake Road and Anil Roy Road. It was a triangular plot my grandfather had bought and developed for his five sons and two daughters. This had been my home until I left for Mumbai. And coming from a one-bedroom flat in Mumbai, my house now looked large and felt strange.

At the exact intersection of the two roads was the drawing room, which was circular. It was beautiful and it gave you a sense of space because of the full windows at one semi-circle. It had cupboards with faces of Bankim Chandra, Sarat

Chandra and Rabindranath Tagore pasted on them. Next to Tagore's bust was a copy of *Gitobitan*. Another wall had photographs of Ram Krishna, Swami Vivekananda and Sharada Ma with garlands around them. Sofas with green and red checked cushions adorned our drawing room. There was a side table with a TV from 1992 that was covered with a flowery cloth. There was large carpet in the middle of the room and a four-poster single bed on one side so it could double up as a bedroom for extra guests.

And in this space sat all the five brothers and their children. My mother sat at the head, respected and admired by most of the family members. And feared by a few.

I walked in and touched everyone's feet. I was expecting a large welcome but it somehow seemed overwhelming. Maybe I was used to so much space and independence that it felt odd. I realized that living with Radha for two years had made me feel like a king in my own house. Now I was just a small prince in a house of kings.

Nandini and Lengtu had met me at the airport and we chatted about Radha all the way home. We knew we couldn't speak about it at home. If anyone got to know I had been in a relationship they would grill me to death. I didn't mention that I was rejected by Meera after that. I was done with women. I didn't want to have anything to do with them for a long time. All I wanted was to take a break, and chill for a month before I found work again.

I met everyone with a hug while one of my uncles said, '*Mishti aano*.' And a platter of sweets was brought out for me. Tea was served and I began to slowly unwind. I sat down and realized there was a girl there whom I hadn't met before.

I presumed she was Huma Mashi's daughter. I hadn't met

most of my cousins for years. The girl was very beautiful. I thought it would have been better if she wasn't my cousin, 'Jodi cousin *na hoto taale bhalo-e hi hoto.*' At least I would have had some entertainment for a month. But my brain took over and calmed my burning loins. It had been too long since I'd had sex. Radha had left me and somewhere I was still wondering if my heart had recovered. We had been together a long time, after all. Maybe it was for the best, but all relationships felt pointless at this point.

I excused myself to go to the kitchen and get myself a glass of water. The family started chatting amongst themselves on a burning political issue. The Bengali war hero Arnab was discussed with great reverence. I was in no mood to participate at this time.

The girl followed me and took a glass of water herself. I decided it would be rude not to strike up a conversation. I mean she was my cousin, after all. I had to at least be polite.

'Hi. Long time, huh?'

'Yes.'

'Are you working?'

She nodded, 'Finished studies. Just joined a firm.'

'What did you study?'

'I did my Master's in English.'

I nodded. How could I figure out how she was related to me? 'So...you are Khokon's sister, no?' I asked.

No.

Bablu?

No.

Chotu?

No.

Silence. Ten seconds. Was this my fat cousin Rinku who had lived with us earlier and moved out to study in the US?

Taaleh. Did you live on the top floor?

No.

Middle floor? Ground floor! You're Tushi aren't you? My God you've changed!

No. I'm not Tushi.

Silence. It dawned on me then that this was a plot executed far better than a *Mission Impossible* movie. She wasn't related to me at all. My mother had pulled off the arranged marriage ploy. I wanted desperately to cut the conversation short and run to my room and lie down. No more women!

'What's your name?'

'Anandita. But you can call me Annie.' That just blew my mind away. The way she said it. The tilt of her head. Her large Bambi eyes. Focus, Obro! No women!

'You're not related to me are you?' I asked, double-checking.

She shook her head and smiled. She had been in on the plot as well. 'I was told that I would meet the most handsome man I've ever seen, and the most daring as well.'

I smiled. Flattery was better than food to a Bengal man's heart. I knew my resolution needed revisiting. But I wanted to take it slow. I didn't want to rush into a relationship or a marriage.

I smiled politely and said, '*Taaleh kalke aamra*...we can meet at, say, Flury's? *Akhon*, I'm tired actually.'

'Sure. Sure. See you tomorrow. Take care,' she said as she turned and walked back into the drawing room while I stood there and checked out her fine ass. Through her tight white kurta I had seen she had a terrific figure that would put even Sunny Leone to shame.

I walked back to my room. The servants had already

placed my bags there and a fresh towel on the bed. I put my wallet and sunglasses on the dressing table. I walked to the window and looked outside. Just then I heard a sound at my door. I turned and saw Anandita standing there. She cleared her throat and asked, 'You didn't tell me what time to meet at Flurys.'

'I don't know. Anytime in the morning?' I suggested, trying to keep it casual and not feel shocked that she had the audacity to find my room and come looking for me. What a forward-thinking woman. She reminded me of someone...

'Eleven?' she said more confidently.

'Okay.'

'Will you call me?'

'Sure.'

'Nandini has my number.'

'Okay.'

'When will you call me?' she asked with a particular tone in her voice.

'Tomorrow.'

'Before or after we meet? Or both times?'

Bloody hell. Men can never win. We don't know why we allow women to dominate us. It's probably because we lust after them. And it overrules our better judgment. I knew I couldn't help it, but I was stuck.

I said a little prayer for all of us, even as Annie became my next clingy girlfriend.

ABOUT THE AUTHOR

Madhuri Banerjee is the bestselling author of five novels. She is also the writer of the successful Bollywood film, *Hate Story 2*. She has a blog on CNN-IBN called Chastity Belt. She has her own production house and is an ad film director. She was a columnist with the *Asian Age* for two years and currently has a column in *Maxim* magazine. She has also won a National Award for her documentary on women's issues called *Between Dualities*. Currently she is the face of Revlon as their Relationship Expert.

She Tweets with the handle @Madhuribanerjee and has over 16,000 followers who love her relationship advice. Her personal blog, www.madhuribanerjee.blogspot.in, has over four lakh views already. She is a world traveller, an avid reader, a coffee addict, an amateur photographer, an Instagram addict, a doting mother, and a fashion advisor.

Her observations of the male species and tales of her personal life in reverse format has made her write this book, a completely different take from any writing she's ever done before!